Andrew Clements

Illustrations by Mark Elliott

Simon & Schuster Books for Young Readers
New York · London · Toronto · Sydney

Also by Andrew Clements

SIMON & SCHUSTER BOOKS FOR YOUNG READERS · An imprint of Simon & Schuster Children's Publishing Division · 1230 Avenue of the Americas, New York, New York 10020 · This book is a work of fiction. Any references to historical events, real people, or real locales are used fictitiously. Other names, characters, places, and incidents are products of the author's imagination, and any resemblance to actual events or locales or persons, living or dead, is entirely coincidental. · Copyright © 2007 by Andrew Clements · All rights reserved, including the right of reproduction in whole or in part in any form. · SIMON & SCHUSTER BOOKS FOR YOUNG READERS is a trademark of Simon & Schuster, Inc. · Book design by Alicia Mikles · The text for this book is set in Bembo. · Manufactured in the United States of America · 10 9 8 7 6 5 4 3 2 1 · Library of Congress Cataloging-in-Publication Data · Clements, Andrew, 1949- · No talking / Andrew Clements.— 1st ed. · p. cm. · Summary: The noisy fifth-grade boys of Laketon Elementary School challenge the equally loud fifth-grade girls to a "no talking" contest. · ISBN-13: 978-1-4169-0983-5 (hardcover : alk. paper) · ISBN-10: 1-4169-0983-4 (hardcover : alk. paper) · [1. Contests—Fiction. 2. Behavior—Fiction. 3. Communication—Fiction. 4. Schools—Fiction.] I. Title. · PZ7.C59118No 2007 · [Fic]—dc22 · 2006031883

FIRST EDITION

For my brother, Matthew Day Clements

CHAPTER 1

ZIPPED

Dave Packer was in the middle of his fourth hour of not talking. He was also in the middle of his social studies class on a Monday morning in the middle of November. And Laketon Elementary School was in the middle of a medium-size town in the middle of New Jersey.

There was a reason Dave was in the middle of his fourth hour of not talking, but this isn't the time to tell about that. This is the time to tell what he figured out in the middle of his social studies class.

Dave figured out that not talking is *extra* hard at school. And the reason? Teachers. Because at 11:35 Mrs. Overby clapped her hands and said, "Class—class! Quiet down!" Then she looked at her list and said, "Dave and Lynsey, you're next."

So Dave nodded at Lynsey and stood up. It was time to present their report about India.

But giving this report would ruin his experiment. Because Dave was trying to keep his mouth shut all day. He wanted to keep his lips zipped right up to the very end of the day, to not say one single word until the last bell rang at ten after three. And the reason Dave had decided to clam up . . . but it still isn't the time to tell about that. This is the time to tell what he did about the report.

Dave and Lynsey walked to the front of the room. Dave was supposed to begin the presentation by telling about the history of India. He looked down at his index cards, looked up at Mrs. Overby, looked out at the class, and he opened his mouth.

But he didn't talk.

He coughed. Dave coughed for about ten seconds. Then he wiped his mouth, looked at his index cards again, looked at Mrs. Overby again, looked at the class again, opened his mouth again, and . . . coughed some more. He coughed and coughed and coughed until his face was bright red and he was all bent over.

Lynsey stood there, feeling helpless. Dave hadn't told her about his experiment, so all she could do was watch—and listen to his horrible coughing. Lynsey's opinion of Dave had never been high, and it sank lower by the second.

Mrs. Overby thought she knew what was happening with Dave. She had seen this before—kids who got so nervous that they made themselves sick rather than talk in front of the class. It surprised her, because Dave wasn't shy at all. Ever. In fact, *none* of this year's fifth graders were the least bit shy or nervous about talking. Ever.

But the teacher took pity, and she said, "You'd better go get some water. You two can give your report later."

Lynsey gave Dave a disgusted look and went back to her desk.

Dave nodded at Mrs. Overby, coughed a few more times for good measure, and hurried out of the room.

And with Dave out in the hall getting a drink, it's the perfect time to tell why he was in the middle of his fourth hour of not talking, and why he had decided to keep quiet in the first place.

GANDHI

When something happens, there's usually a simple explanation. But that simple explanation is almost never the full story.

Here's the simple explanation anyway: Dave had decided to stop talking for a whole day because of something he'd read in a book.

See? Very simple, very clear. But it's not the whole story.

So here's a little more.

Dave and a partner had to prepare a report on India—not a long one, just some basic facts. Something about the history, something about the government, something about the land and the industry, something about the Indian people and their culture. Five minutes or less.

Dave's report partner was Lynsey Burgess, and neither one of them was happy about that—there

were some boy-girl problems at Laketon Elementary School. But this isn't the time to tell about that.

Even though Dave and Lynsey had to *give* their report together, they both agreed that they did *not* want to *prepare* it together. So they divided the topics in half, and each worked alone.

Dave was a good student, and he had found two books about India, and he had checked them out of the library. He hadn't read both books, not completely—he wasn't *that* good a student. But he had read parts of both books.

Dave thought the most interesting section in each book was the part about how India became independent, how the country broke away from England to become a free nation—sort of like the United States did.

And Dave thought the most interesting person in the story of India's independence was Mahatma Gandhi.

Dave was amazed by Gandhi. This one skinny little man practically pushed the whole British army out of India all by himself. But he didn't use weapons or violence. He fought with words and ideas. It was an incredible story, all of it true.

And in one of the books, Dave read this about Gandhi:

For many years, one day each week
Gandhi did not speak at all. Gandhi
believed this was a way to bring
order to his mind.

Dave read that bit of information on Thursday afternoon, and he read it again on Sunday night as he prepared for his oral report. And it made him wonder what that would be like—to go a whole day without saying a single word. And Dave began to wonder if not talking would bring order to *his* mind too.

In fact, Dave wondered what that meant, "to bring order to his mind." Could something as simple as not talking change the way your mind worked? Seemed like it must have been good for Gandhi. But what would it do for a regular kid in New Jersey?

Would not talking make him . . . smarter? Would he finally understand fractions? If he had more order in his mind, would he be able to look at a sentence and *see* which word was an adverb—instead of just guessing? And how about sports? Would someone with a more orderly mind be a better baseball player?

Powerful questions.

So Dave decided to zip his lip and give it a try.

Was it hard for him to keep quiet? You bet, especially at first, like when he got to the bus stop, where his friends were arguing about why the Jets had lost to the Patriots. But Dave had learned quickly that by nodding and smiling, by frowning and shrugging, by shaking his head, by giving a thumbs-up or a high five, or even by just putting his hands in his coat pockets and turning away, not talking was possible. And by the time he'd ridden the bus to school, Dave had gotten pretty good at fitting in without speaking up.

There. That explains what's going on a little better. And it's probably enough, at least for the moment. But there's more. There's *always* more.

And now we're back in class on Monday with Dave, who got through the rest of social studies without saying a word. And when the bell rang at the end of the period, it was time for fifth-grade lunch.

More than a hundred and twenty-five kids began hurrying toward the cafeteria. And by the time they got there, the fifth graders were already talking like crazy—all except one.

CHAPTER 3

INSULTS

"**I**f you had to shut up for five minutes, I bet the whole top of your head would explode!" As those words flew out of his mouth, Dave had two thoughts.

First, he thought, *Darn it!*—because he remembered he'd been trying not to talk at all.

And his second thought was, *Gandhi probably wouldn't have said that.* Because it wasn't a very nice thing to say.

But that's what Dave said, and he said it to Lynsey Burgess, and there was a reason he said it.

So it's time to back up a little and explain.

Dave had gotten through the lunch line without a peep. He had pointed at the pizza plate, then pointed at the fruit cup. He had nodded for "yes, please" and shook his head for "no, thanks." He had grabbed some milk from the cooler and flashed his lunch pass at Mrs. Vitelli. And he had smiled a lot.

No talking? No problem.

Then he'd sat down at a table with some of his friends, just like always. But instead of jumping into the conversation, Dave had kept a pleasant look on his face, and he'd kept his mouth full of food.

No talking? No problem.

And because he wasn't talking, Dave had focused all his energy on listening.

Listening at the lunch table, really *listening*, was a brand-new experience for him. Because most of the time Dave was a loudmouth.

See? There's something more about Dave. And it makes Dave's reaction to Gandhi make more sense. Because if Dave himself was a loudmouth, a real tongue-flapper, then someone like Gandhi who could keep completely quiet would seem that much more amazing.

Because Dave really did love to talk. He could talk and talk and talk about almost anything—baseball, cars, dinosaurs, rock hunting, soccer, snowboarding, waterskiing, favorite books, best football players, camping, canoeing, PlayStation, Nintendo, Xbox, comic books, TV shows, movies—you name it. Dave had a long, long list of interests, and he had plenty of opinions.

Plus, talking always made Dave feel like he was in charge. It was sort of like being a police officer out in the middle of traffic. As long as *he* did the talking, the traffic went the way *he* wanted it to. This was especially useful if insults started flying around. When it came to dishing out the put-downs, Dave was a pro.

But this lunchtime, all the *other* loudmouths were getting a chance to spout off.

So Dave had chewed his pizza, and sipped his milk, and listened. And after a minute or two he began listening to Lynsey Burgess. But only because he couldn't help it.

Even though she was sitting behind him at the next table, and even though the cafeteria was almost bursting with noise, Lynsey had a sharp voice, the kind that cuts like a hacksaw.

". . . so I said, 'Are you serious?' and she said, 'What's wrong with you?' and I said, 'Because I saw it first,' and I did, and it was a great color for me, because my hair's brown, and her hair's that mousy blond color, but her mom was right there in the store, so she picked it up and took it over to her, and her mom bought it! Can you *believe* that? She *knew* I wanted that sweater more than anything, and she bought it anyway. And then? After school on Friday at soccer

12

practice? She *smiled* at me, like she wanted to be friends or something—as *if*! Can you *believe* that?"

No, Dave couldn't believe it. He couldn't believe that anyone could flap and yap her mouth so fast, and say so many words, and be so boring and stupid-sounding, all at the same time. He took another bite of pizza and tried to stop listening, but Lynsey was just getting warmed up.

". . . because then, she comes over *after* practice? And she says, 'Here, this is for you,' and she tries to *give* me the sweater. So I pull my hands away like she's holding a dead skunk or something, and I say, 'You think I want *that*? That thing is so ugly, I would *never* wear that!' And she says, 'Oh'—just like that—just, 'Oh'—and she walks away with the sweater. Except now, I wish I hadn't said that, because it really is the *best* color, and it's really soft. . . ."

By this point, Dave was wishing he had an iPod. Because if he had one, and if it hadn't been against school rules, he could have plugged up both his ears and cranked the volume. Anything to get away from the sound of Lynsey's voice.

". . . because once I tried wearing this sweater that was made of wool? And it made my neck itch *so* much, like, I couldn't even wear it for two minutes, but it was okay, because then my mom found this turtleneck way down in the bottom of my dresser, and I'd forgotten I even had it, and it was pink, so then I put that on first, and then the sweater was fine, because, really, it was like the two colors went together *perfectly*, almost like a picture in a magazine. Because last week in *Teen People*? Jenna and Lori and Keith were at this party, like, in Hollywood or somewhere? And Jenna had on a sweater that was almost like that wool one I have, and she was wearing these . . ."

And that was the moment when Dave completely forgot about keeping silent, and he turned around and almost shouted, "If you had to shut up for five minutes, I bet the whole top of your head would explode!"

And Dave was glad he'd said it, even if it wasn't nice, and even though it ended his experiment. Because after he said it, Lynsey stopped talking.

But the quiet only lasted about three seconds.

Lynsey said, "Is your *cough* all better? Because I thought I just heard a whiny little voice." She and her friends stared at Dave. "Did you say something?"

"Yeah, I did," he said. "I *said*, I bet if you had to shut up for five minutes, the top of your head would explode. Like a volcano. From all the hot gas that usually comes out of your mouth. When you talk

14

and talk and talk and never stop talking. Yeah. That's what I said. To you."

Lynsey tilted her head and looked at Dave, sort of the way a bird looks at a bug it's about to eat.

"Oh, like there's something *wrong* with talking? You never have any trouble with *yourself* blabbing and blabbing every day. We've all *heard* you." And the other girls nodded and made faces.

"Well," Dave said, "talking's okay, when there's stuff worth saying."

Lynsey said, "*Ohhh*—so *boys* can say things like, 'Hey, did you hear this guy got traded to that team, and that guy got traded to this team, and, hey, he hit real good last year, and, ooh yeah, he can really catch!' Boys can talk and talk like that, but girls can't talk about clothes sometimes? Is *that* it?"

Dave said, "No . . . but I don't talk the way you talk, like, for a million minutes in a row without stopping. And . . . and . . ."

Dave was hunting for something strong to say, a real punch line, something that would shut Lynsey up and end this conversation. So he said, ". . . and anyway, boys *never* talk as much as girls do, ever!"

Please take a careful look at that last thing Dave just said.

Because with this particular group of fifth

graders, *that* was a dangerous thing to say.

And now is a good time to tell a little more about the fifth-grade boys and the fifth-grade girls at Laketon Elementary School—to explain why it was a bad idea for Dave to say what he just said.

Because Dave should have kept his mouth shut.

He really should have.

CHAPTER 4

COOTIES

When little Dave Packer and all the other kids his age first showed up to begin kindergarten together, it was sort of like they were new recruits joining the army.

And kindergarten was sort of like basic training camp, except the teachers were a lot nicer than army drill instructors.

After nine long months together in kindergarten, Dave and the other new recruits were allowed to quit the army—but only for the summer. Because in September they all had to re-enlist for first grade.

And after first grade, they marched through second grade together, then third, and so on, right through the grades. Together. A few kids moved away, and a couple of new kids arrived, but Dave and those original kindergarten recruits stayed together, year after year. And they began to grow up. Together.

At most elementary schools, by the time a group gets to fifth grade, the boys have stopped thinking that all the girls have cooties, and the girls have stopped thinking that all the boys have cooties. And that's the way it should be—to outgrow that stuff.

For some groups, it's easy. The kids grow up a little bit, and they all learn that everyone's a real person, and some of those persons are boys and some are girls, and suddenly everyone gets along just fine, person to person. No more cooties.

However, some groups of kids cling to those cooties a little too long. The boys avoid the girls, and the girls avoid the boys, and everyone keeps seeing cooties everywhere. And, sadly, that's the way it was with most of the fifth-grade kids at Laketon Elementary School.

Of course, the fifth graders didn't actually use the word "cooties" anymore—that would have sounded like baby talk. They used words like "dumb" or "gross" or "immature" or "annoying." But a cootie by any other name is still a cootie.

And even worse, Dave and Lynsey were the king and queen of the fifth-grade cootie-clingers. Dave had zero tolerance for girls, and Lynsey had less-than-zero tolerance for boys.

And *that's* why Dave should have kept his mouth shut.

Now it's time to get back to the action in the lunchroom, because when Lynsey heard Dave say "boys never talk as much as girls do," she felt like all girls everywhere had been insulted, slapped in the face by a dumb, gross, immature, annoying boy. And she hadn't forgotten what Dave had already said, about the top of her head blowing off. Because of hot gas.

Lynsey wasn't the kind of person who forgives and forgets an insult. She was the kind of person who remembers. And then gets even.

CHAPTER 5

THE CONTEST

L ynsey narrowed her eyes and hissed, "You take that back!"

Dave shrugged. "Take what back? That girls are big blabberheads all the time? No way—because they *are*! Everybody knows that."

It's a shame to have to report this, but Dave actually believed what he was saying. And in his ignorant but creative young mind, an idea sparked to life.

Before Lynsey or any of her friends could say something back, Dave said, "And there's a way to *prove* that girls talk way more than boys. Unless you're afraid of some competition, you and your noisy friends."

"Afraid?" Lynsey said, looking around at the girls. "We're not afraid of anything—except catching whatever made *you* so stupid."

The girls giggled, but Dave ignored the insult, completely caught up by his new idea. He waved his hands to quiet them down. "Okay, here's the deal: a whole day of no talking at school. Not in class, not in the halls, not on the playground, nowhere. No talking at all. And it's a contest—boys against girls. Whichever side talks less, wins."

Lynsey made a face. "No talking? At school? That's impossible."

Dave had an advantage here. He had just spent almost four hours without saying a word. At school. So he had some experience, and he felt like he knew what he was talking about.

He grinned and said, "Maybe it's impossible for a *girl* to be quiet. But I bet the boys can do it. Or at least, we can do it better than the girls."

Lynsey said, "But, like, what if a teacher looked right at you and asked a question, then what?"

Dave grinned and said, "You could always . . . cough."

Lynsey's mouth dropped open, and then she glared at him. "You did that coughing in social studies *on purpose*? You are *so* immature!"

Dave shrugged. "It was sort of a test. And it worked. But if every kid in fifth grade coughed every time a teacher asked a question? *That* would *not* work."

Lynsey sniffed. "Well, *I* say that this whole idea is . . . childish. Silly and childish."

"It's okay if you don't want to," Dave said. "It was just an idea. I mean, I can see why you'd be afraid, since you're a girl and all. And since you *have* to talk every other second. No problem. Sorry I interrupted you. Just keep talking to your friends there. You were talking about something important, weren't you? That special sweater, right? Go ahead, talk. You girls go on and talk and talk and talk all you want to."

Lynsey pressed her lips together and glared at Dave, her eyes narrowed to slits. "You are the most annoying little—" She stopped mid-insult and folded her arms. "All right," she said. "Let's work out the rules. Right now. If a teacher talks to you, what then?"

"You answer," Dave said.

"How many words can you use?" she asked.

Dave smiled. "Let's make it . . . ten words—in case you and your friends need to tell a teacher about some new clothes you got."

"Stop trying to be funny. Because you're *not*," Lynsey said. "Make the limit four words. If you answer with more than four words in a row, the extras count."

Dave shook his head. "Four's still too easy. Let's make it a three-word limit. And every illegal word is one point—*against* your team."

"Duh," said Lynsey. "Like I needed you to explain that!"

"So it's a three-word limit?" Dave said.

"Three," said Lynsey, "and you can answer teachers, or the principal . . ."

". . . or any grown-up at school," said Dave. "Like the custodian."

"Or the nurse," added Lynsey. Because she wasn't about to let Dave Packer have the last word about anything.

"What about contractions?" she asked.

"What about 'em?" Dave said.

"Does a contraction count as one word or two?"

Dave didn't let it show in his face, but he was impressed by Lynsey's question—that she was able to think so far ahead and figure out that words like "won't" or "isn't" could cause a scorekeeping problem. And right away, Dave was just as impressed with himself, because he understood how to answer her question with a question of his own.

He said, "If you go find a dictionary, can you look up the word 'won't'?"

Lynsey nodded. "Of course you can."

"Then it's a word—one word," said Dave. "Any other questions?"

And now it was Lynsey's turn to hide her

thoughts, because she was impressed with Dave's answer. He was still *very* annoying, but his answer seemed right, plus he'd explained his reasoning clearly. But she didn't get carried away with good feelings about Dave. He was still a miserable, unpleasant boy who was forcing her to get involved in a pointless contest.

It's also a shame to have to report this, but Lynsey was just as proud and stubborn as Dave. And since he had pushed her into this fight, she felt it was her duty to push back—and she saw the perfect way to do it.

She turned away and whispered something to the girls at her lunch table, and when they all nodded their heads, she turned back to Dave. She gestured toward her friends and said, "*We* want to make this contest harder. How about this: no talking at home, either. Or on the school bus, or anywhere else. No talking at all—except for what we already decided. Not even to parents. And let's make the contest last for *two* days instead of one—two twenty-four-hour days in a row. Unless you think that's too *hard*."

Dave shrugged. "Fine, no problem. Except . . . how do we keep track of all the mess-ups when you and your friends start gabbing at home?"

"You mean, when the *boys* cheat?" said Lynsey.

"Simple. We'll have to use the honor system when we're not at school. It's the only way. We all keep track of our own mistakes. And report them. *Honestly*. Except I don't know if the *boys* can be trusted. Have any boys even *heard* of the honor system? I *know* you can trust the girls."

"Don't worry about us," Dave said.

Lynsey tossed her head. "So when does the contest start? The girls can be ready by tomorrow. At lunchtime. Unless that's too soon for the boys. Do you need more time to get organized? Like a week? Or *two* weeks?"

"Very funny," said Dave. "We'll start Tuesday, tomorrow. At the beginning of lunch. And it's not over until Thursday . . . how about at twelve fifteen? That'll be the middle of lunch period." Lynsey nodded, and Dave went on. "I'll be the official score-keeper for our side, and you keep track for the girls. And no cheating. Okay?"

Lynsey nodded again. "Agreed." She held out her hand.

Dave looked at it like it was covered with slime. "What?" he said.

Lynsey wrinkled her nose. "It's *revolting*, but we have to shake on it—so *you* won't try to back out."

Dave shook, and then made a show of wiping his

hand on his pants, which got a big laugh from the five or six other boys who had witnessed the ceremony.

And as Dave turned and went into a huddle with the guys at his lunch table, Lynsey did the same with the girls at her table.

The contest was on.

CHAPTER 6

TEAMWORK

The boys Dave ate lunch with were his best friends. He looked around at them and grinned after he'd explained the rules. "Cool contest, huh?"

Todd shook his head. "I'm not doing this—it's dumb. Who wants to not talk? Besides, it's impossible, like she said."

"You think girls *can* stop talking, but boys *can't*?" Dave asked. "So you're just giving up without a fight? Is that it?"

Todd said, "Well, no . . . but it's still a stupid idea."

"So what?" said Dave. "It's a *contest*, and the boys are gonna win it, okay? So listen. First, we've got to tell every guy. Everybody *has* to be with us on this. Tim Flanagan was absent in homeroom this morning. I'll call him, in case he's coming back tomorrow. And you all have to do that too, figure out who else isn't here. And if you don't have a number, call me at home tonight, 'cause my mom has a school directory. And every fifth-grade boy who's here at school has to be told. Today. Okay?"

Jason said, "But really, not talking? For two days? Like . . . how?"

Dave pulled an index card from his pocket. On the back of his India report he wrote the word "Easy." He held it up, showing it to all the boys.

Then he said, "Did I just talk?"

"No," said Jason.

Dave said, "Keep watching."

He shook his head.

Then he nodded at them.

Then he smiled.

Then he frowned and showed his teeth and growled like a dog.

"I didn't talk, right? But you *got* what I said. Not talking just means . . . not talking. It'll probably be fun—but even if it's not, it's a *contest*. Against the girls. And we're gonna win it, right? And tell all the guys to practice short sentences. Three words or less."

Jim said, "You bug me!"

Jason said, "Your breath smells!"

Richard said, "Look, it's Batman!—hey, is Batman one word or two?"

And the sentences kept coming, each boy trying to be the goofiest.

"Guys," Dave said. "Guys, c'mon. We've only got fourteen minutes before next period. *All* the fifth-grade boys are right here at lunch—it's the perfect chance to tell everyone. And I hate to tell you, but the girls are already ahead of us."

The boys hushed, and looked around.

Lynsey, Anna, Emily, Taron—all the friends who'd been sitting at the next table were fanning out through the cafeteria, talking to every girl in sight. And Hannah and Karin were heading for the door to the playground.

Dave said, "Everybody know what you have to say to our team?"

The boys looked back at him and nodded, each face deadly serious now.

"All right, then," Dave said. "Let's do this."

CHAPTER 7

THE UNSHUSHABLES

Since Dave and Lynsey had been almost shouting at each other in the middle of the cafeteria, you might think that a lot of the other fifth graders in the room would have tuned in and paid attention to the commotion. You might think that a lot of the kids in the lunchroom already knew about the contest.

But if you thought that, you'd be wrong.

And you'd be wrong because you don't understand just how *loud*, how incredibly *noisy* it was in the cafeteria during fifth-grade lunch. And not just on this one day. It was noisy during fifth-grade lunch *every* day.

And it wasn't noisy only at lunch. *Anywhere* a bunch of these fifth graders got together, the talking got out of hand.

That's why it's time to tell a little more about

this particular set of fifth-grade kids.

Because there's more to tell. There's *always* more.

A school system really is a little like the army—remember? About how kindergarten is sort of like basic training camp?

Because kindergarten was where Dave and the other new recruits first learned the rules. They learned when to sit and when to stand, when to talk and when to hush, when to walk and when to run, when to eat, and nap, and play, and sing, and draw, and everything else.

Because every system needs rules—no rules, no system.

Most of the rules made perfect sense to Dave and the new recruits, especially rules like this: no fighting, no bullying, no shoving, no spitting, no biting, no stealing, no vandalism, no cutting in line, no snowball throwing, and so on.

For most kids, the really serious rules like that weren't hard at all. Those were the easy ones.

The toughest rules were ones like, "No running in the halls."

Hard.

"No disorderly behavior on the buses."

Also hard.

"No candy or chewing gum."

Very hard.

But nowhere in the forty-four-page Laketon Elementary School Handbook did it actually say, "No whispering, chatting, talking, calling out, yelling, or shouting in classrooms, in the hallways, in the auditorium, or in the lunchroom."

True, there *was* a rule about paying attention in class. And there *was* a rule about being respectful. And there *was* a rule about being courteous at all times.

And Dave and his classmates obeyed those rules—or at least, they *thought* they did. It's just that they all seemed to think they could talk *and* be courteous—at the same time. And they all seemed to think they could talk *and* pay attention—at the same time.

Because none of these kids really meant to be disrespectful or disobedient or discourteous. But none of them wanted to stop talking. Ever.

In fact, this group of kids had been given a nickname by the teachers at Laketon Elementary School, and the name had stuck with them ever since they had all been in first grade together. They were "The Unshushables."

If Laketon Elementary School had *really* been like the army, then sometime—probably during second grade—Dave and Lynsey and all the other recruits would have been lined up out on the playground on a cold, rainy morning, and a gruff man with short hair and shiny shoes would have walked up and down in front of them, shouting right into their faces. And he would have shouted something like this:

"YOU DRIVE ME *CRAZY*! You call yourselves *STUDENTS*? You are a MISERABLE *MOB*! You are LOUD, UNdisciplined, and I WILL not tolerate your NOISE! When you walk in MY hallways, you do not SHOUT! You do not WAVE and YELL and HOOT when you see your friends. At an assembly in MY school, you do NOT whisper and giggle and point and wave and laugh at your own silly jokes! And when you come to MY lunchroom, it is NOT a free-for-all festival of flap-jawed jibber-jabber! Lunch is a time to SIT and be QUIET and EAT. I am going to TEACH you little motormouth MONSTERS proper school MANNERS if it is THE LAST

THING I DO! DO I MAKE MYSELF
CLEAR?"
   "YES, SIR!"
"QUIETER!"
"Yes, sir!"

But, of course, Laketon Elementary School wasn't
the army.

However, with Mrs. Abigail Hiatt in charge,
sometimes it felt that way. She was a tall woman with
a long face, curly gray hair, and bright blue eyes, and
she had been the principal at Laketon Elementary
School for the past thirteen years.

She gave careful orders, set precise goals, and she
demanded results from her teachers, from her office
staff, from her custodians, from her cafeteria workers,
and from her students and their parents, too. Her
school never went over its budget, never missed its
academic targets, and the place never felt loose or
sloppy or disorderly.

Under Mrs. Hiatt's watchful eye, group after
group of children had wandered into Laketon
Elementary School as aimless little kindergartners
and marched out six years later as perfectly disci-
plined young students. Under Mrs. Hiatt's leadership, the place ran like clockwork.

And then the Unshushables came along. In all her years as principal she had never known a group of kids like this.

And for the past five years, Mrs. Hiatt had been trying to make these kids obey the simplest school rule of all: no talking—except when it's allowed.

Year after year, memos had been sent home to the parents of Dave and his classmates about too much shouting on the school buses.

Year after year, Dave's grade had been told how to behave before every assembly.

Year after year, all their teachers had stood out in the hallways to try to keep the noise down before and after school, and especially at lunchtime.

This group had even been given a separate lunch period for the past three years in a row: third-grade lunch, fourth-grade lunch, and this year, fifth-grade lunch. Mrs. Hiatt had made that decision. She didn't want the noisy behavior of this group to infect the other children at her school. Because year after year, the Unshushables lived up to their nickname.

To be honest, a few of this year's fifth-grade teachers had already given up. They didn't have any real hope of changing these kids. They were just trying to cope. Because it was already November, so in six short months the Unshushables would be gone forever, moved along to the junior high, and next year Laketon Elementary School would be quieter. *Much* quieter.

But Mrs. Hiatt had not given up, not by a long shot. She still had over half a year with these kids, and she intended to use that time.

Every day the principal stalked the fifth-grade hall. *"You there*—stop shouting!"

At every assembly, she glared. "And I don't want to hear even a *whisper* from our fifth graders, is that clear?"

At every fifth-grade lunch, she walked around the cafeteria with a big red plastic bullhorn, and when the noise became unbearable, she pulled the trigger and bellowed, "STUDENTS! YOU ARE TALKING TOO LOUD!"

Mrs. Hiatt felt sure that this constant reminding *had* to be having an effect on these kids . . . how could it not? After all, these were good kids . . . right? They *had* to be making progress . . . didn't they?

She knew she was being very stern with them, but it was for their own good. And Mrs. Hiatt felt sure that sooner or later, these kids would grow up a little—and quiet down a lot.

• • •

And now it's time to tell what happened in the middle of the second Tuesday in November during Dave Packer's final year at Laketon Elementary School.

It was two minutes before fifth-grade lunch, and the principal was ready, just like always. Mrs. Hiatt had checked to be sure that the other teacher who had fifth-grade lunch duty wasn't out sick or at a meeting. Because it wasn't good to try to manage fifth-grade lunch all by yourself.

And, just like always, she had ordered Mr. Lipton, the custodian, to stay in the cafeteria today until 12:40. Because with this group, the more grown-ups around, the better.

And Mrs. Hiatt had double-checked the batteries in her red plastic bullhorn. Because it wasn't good to have a dead bullhorn during fifth-grade lunch.

Then the bell rang, and as classroom doors along the fifth-grade hall flew open, Mrs. Hiatt could hear them coming, all of them, already calling to each other as locker doors clanged open and banged shut, already talking a mile a minute, already laughing and whooping and shouting, streaming down the hallway toward the cafeteria, an unshushable wave of energy and excitement and noise . . . *so much noise!*

Mrs. Hiatt took her position at the center of the cafeteria and braced herself. She was ready for today's lunchroom battle, ready to change chaos into order, ready for anything these kids could dish out.

But nothing could have prepared her for what happened next.

CHAPTER 8

SCIENCE FICTION

It was four minutes into the fifth-grade lunch period, and Mrs. Hiatt was pretty sure that any second now, her alarm clock was going to start making that awful sound—**BRRAP! BRRAP! BRRAP! BRRAP!**

Because the principal was almost certain that she was still at home in her own comfy bed, dreaming away. She *had* to be dreaming. But no, she looked at her watch and it showed the same time as the large clock above the stage in the school cafeteria—12:04.

On any other day Mrs. Hiatt would have already used her bullhorn at least once, because when half the fifth graders were standing in the food line, and the other half were in the milk line or rushing toward their seats, there was always a terrific burst of yelling and calling out and wild chatter—sort of like feeding time at the zoo.

Not today.

There was no talking at all. Not one word. Over one hundred twenty-five children milling around the lunchroom, and not a peep from any of them.

Today the principal could hear the clattering of the worn-out motor in the milk cooler. And she could hear the kitchen workers talking softly to each other. And she could hear the children's feet on the tile floor, shuffling along through the lines.

The quiet almost frightened her. Mrs. Hiatt felt like she was in a scene from a creepy science fiction movie.

She actually liked a good scary movie now and then, but she did *not* like the ideas in her mind at this moment. Because it seemed like aliens had possessed these fifth graders and zapped their brains. Or maybe some strange creature had nipped off all their tongues—nothing left but little stubs that couldn't make a sound.

The principal shivered. Then she noticed a girl staring at her. Mrs. Hiatt realized she must have had a strange look on her face.

As the girl sat down with her lunch tray, Mrs. Hiatt forced herself to smile, and said, "Hi there, Sheila. How are you today?" Her voice almost echoed in the quiet lunchroom.

Every boy in the milk line turned and stared at

Sheila. The girls turned and looked too.

Sheila gulped, gave the principal a nervous smile, and, speaking softly and slowly, she said, "Fine, thank you."

Mrs. Hiatt turned toward the milk line, and all the kids looked away. Silently.

And again, the principal felt like she was in the middle of a science fiction movie.

It suddenly seemed silly to be standing there in a silent room with her huge red plastic bullhorn. So Mrs. Hiatt walked over to the playground door, where Mrs. Escobar was standing. She tried to look as casual as possible, tried to act like it was perfectly normal for the lunchroom to be stone silent except for the clattering of plates and the squeaking of sneakers on the waxed floor.

The principal set the bullhorn on the floor by the wall and whispered to Mrs. Escobar, "What in the world is going on here?"

Mrs. Escobar whispered back, "I have no idea. But it's something weird, that's for sure."

Mrs. Hiatt did not like this feeling, this feeling that something strange, something new was happening. Because this new activity was happening at her school, and no one had asked for her permission. This new activity was unauthorized.

Mrs. Hiatt didn't simply *like* being in charge of her own school. She felt like she *needed* to be in charge.

And that's why she felt like she had to say something, do something, to break the spell. So she stepped away from the wall and in a loud voice she said, "Good afternoon, fifth graders. Are you enjoying your lunchtime today?"

All the kids looked at each other. The whole room seemed to take a deep breath, and then almost everyone said, "Yes, Mrs. Hiatt."

And then silence again.

After an awkward few seconds, the principal said, "It's so *quiet* in here today. I'm very . . . impressed. With your good behavior."

Some kids smiled, some nodded. But no one said a word.

Mrs. Hiatt said, "Is there some special reason why no one's talking today?"

The whole room went still. Even the chewing stopped.

No hands went up, and no one answered her question.

But Mrs. Hiatt was a keen observer, and in that sudden stillness she noticed something. Right after she asked her question, it seemed like almost every boy looked at Dave Packer, who was standing beside the milk cooler. And it seemed like almost every girl took a quick look at Lynsey Burgess, who was just sitting down at a table.

And the principal thought, *That's odd.*

But the whole situation was odd. Very odd. And now it seemed like the room was stuck in a complete calm, as if all the kids had even stopped breathing.

Everyone was waiting to see what she was going to do next.

After a few more seconds of suspense, Mrs. Hiatt cleared her throat and said, "Well, students, please enjoy the rest of your lunchtime."

And the cafeteria came back to life. Silently.

CHAPTER 9

THE RIGHT WORD

As Dave sat down at a lunch table with his friends, he couldn't get the grin off his face. He was having so much fun he could hardly chew his first bite of grilled cheese. And he didn't like chewing right now because chewing made noise, and when he munched he couldn't hear the silence.

The *silence*—Dave thought it was amazing.

And watching Mrs. Hiatt try to figure out what was going on? That was amazing too. It was like they had trapped her in a force field. And she couldn't get out of it, because the silence filled the cafeteria.

Dave looked around, and he saw the same amazement on the faces of some other kids. They were all thinking about the same thing. Together.

Then suddenly: "Hey, give it back!"

There was a gasp as every boy and girl in the

room sucked in a breath, and all heads turned to see where those words had come from.

And there at the ice cream freezer, Ed Kesey had one hand over his mouth while his other hand reached for a cherry Popsicle that Bryan DelGreco had grabbed.

Dave swung around and looked at Lynsey.

Lynsey knew a lot of kids were watching her, but she pretended not to notice. She slowly reached into her back pocket, slowly pulled out a pen and a small red notebook, slowly opened the cover, and slowly made four little marks on the first page.

And as she flipped the notebook shut, Lynsey looked right at Dave and gave him a big smile.

Just like that, and the girls were ahead by four points.

But Dave wasn't worried. The contest had barely begun. There were two whole days to go.

Dave was absolutely sure that the next forty-eight hours were going to be very . . . *interesting.* And he thought, *Is that the right word? How about . . . fascinating? No, more like . . . exciting. Yeah—exciting!*

Then Dave happened to glance at Mrs. Hiatt. And he could tell from the look on the principal's face that she had been watching everything—the way Ed had shouted those words and then covered his mouth, the way all the other kids had reacted, the way Lynsey had marked her notebook.

And at that exact moment the principal turned and locked eyes with Dave. She stared right at him, with her eyebrows all bunched up in a puzzled knot.

Dave quickly looked down at his lunch tray, and as he did, a new word popped into his mind. And he was pretty sure this one was also going to be a good word to describe the next few days: *dangerous.*

CHAPTER 10

RECESS

M rs. Marlow was the fifth-grade science teacher, and it was her day for outdoor recess duty. As she was gulping down a quick lunch in the teachers' room, Mr. Lipton, the custodian, stuck his head in the door and said, "Anybody want to see a miracle? Go check out the cafeteria. The fifth graders aren't talking today—not even whispering. It's like a funeral in there."

But Mrs. Marlow didn't have a moment to spare. She finished her lunch, grabbed her coat, and hurried outside to the playground through the gym.

Even without the heads-up from the custodian, it wouldn't have taken her long to figure out that something was different at outside recess today. Every teacher knows the sound of a normal, happy playground at lunchtime—kids talking and yelling and chasing, and all the arguments about who's it and who's out and who ran faster.

Not today. Mrs. Marlow could tell that a whole layer of spoken sound was missing. Gone. Absent.

Except . . . not completely. Because the kids did make some slipups during their first wordless recess.

Allie Bedford got caught whispering to Lena Henderson by the swing set, and when a group of boys stood and shook their fingers at her, she held up eight fingers to show how many illegal words she had said.

Christina Farley didn't have to confess, because half the kids on the playground heard exactly what she said, loud and clear. She stomped her feet, stuck out her tongue at Rachel Morgan, and then shouted, "You're a terrible friend, and you lie, and you're selfish, and I don't care how many words this is! And you're *mean,* too!"

Which was twenty-three words.

Christina's goof, plus the eight words Allie whispered, meant that Dave got to record thirty-one points against the girls on his official score sheet, which wasn't as fancy as Lynsey's red notebook—just a couple of folded index cards stuffed in his pocket.

But the boys weren't perfect either.

Scott Vickers booted a kickball down the third-base line, and when two boys made the "foul ball" motion, he yelled, "Foul? Are you *crazy*? No *way*! That ball was fair!" And Scott would have kept on yelling, but Bill Harkness tackled him and clamped a hand over his mouth—which Scott bit, but not hard enough to make Bill yell any words.

That incident cost the boys ten points.

And then there was the first case of trickery. Katie Edison snuck up behind Jeremy Stephens, who was standing by the sliding board, tapped him on the shoulder, and when he turned his head, she gave him a big, noisy kiss on the cheek.

Jeremy howled and wiped his face and flew into a fit of cootie-itis. "Eeew, *YUCK!* Why did you *do* that? That was so *gross*! *YUCK!* Help me get this stuff off my face!"

Which was twenty more points for the girls. Plus Katie actually enjoyed her sneak attack—she'd had a top secret crush on Jeremy for two months.

Even though there were only a few word blasts, it certainly wasn't quiet out there, and it got noisier and noisier as the end of recess got closer. That's because everyone began to realize that this was not a contest to see who could be silent. It was just about not talking. Sounds were allowed—as long as they weren't words.

Dave was near the door of the gym and began whistling. He was instantly joined by four other boys. They whistled every song they could think of—"Row, Row, Row Your Boat"; "Now I Know My ABCs"; "London Bridge Is Falling Down"; Barney's "Marching Song"; the *Star Wars* theme song; "Old MacDonald Had a Farm"; "I've Been Working on the Railroad"; "Rubber Ducky"—on and on. The whistling was mostly off-key, but it was a grand performance anyway, with lots of clapping and hooting between tunes.

Somewhere near the middle of the whistling concert, six or seven girls began screaming. These were not the kind of screams that make grown-ups come running. They were just an ugly assortment of squeals and yelps and shrieks that everyone else found very annoying. Spaced out around the edge of the playground, the girls bounced their high-pitched sounds around like a beach ball at a baseball stadium: "EeeeOww!" "OooWhee!" "WooHoooh!" "Yeeyeeyeeyeee!" They made lots of noise, but they weren't talking.

Some other girls were jumping double Dutch, and since they couldn't chant the rhymes, the kids who weren't jumping or turning the ropes clapped out the rhythm of the words with their hands.

The quietest activity involved four girls who had a printed folder that showed how to use American Sign Language. They sat in a circle on the ground and practiced their hand signals.

And to round out the soundscape, Bradley Lang and Tyler Rennert were cruising around the playground bothering as many girls as possible by making all sorts of mouth sounds—clicks, pops, roars, quacks, barks, burps, and especially those loud bathroom noises created by putting the palms of both hands over the mouth, puffing up the cheeks, and blooping out a blast of air.

Mrs. Marlow could see there was plenty of activity, but those high-pitched playground voices, all that buzz and chatter and calling out, all that was definitely missing. There was no mistaking it: These kids were not talking, which would have been unusual for any bunch of students. For *this* group of kids, the custodian had called it right: It was practically a miracle.

But why? There had to be a reason they were all acting this way. And as a science-minded person, Mrs. Marlow was curious.

So, as she stood there thinking, Mrs. Marlow

began to adjust her afternoon lesson plan. Because in about ten minutes, twenty-six of these fifth graders would be sitting in her room, ready for science class.

And there was nothing Mrs. Marlow liked better than a good experiment.

CHAPTER 11

QUESTIONS
AND ANSWERS

In all her years of teaching—seventeen in total—Mrs. Marlow had never walked into a quieter classroom full of students. It was a new experience for her.

It was also new for the kids.

Dave watched Mrs. Marlow go to the front of the room and pick up her attendance book. The teacher looked at the list of names in the book, looked up and down the rows of the class, looked at the book again, and said, "I thought maybe I was in the wrong room. Pretty quiet in here today. Can someone tell me why?"

No hands went up.

But Mrs. Marlow was watching for anything that might give her a clue about this unusual behavior.

And after her question, she saw a few sly glances between kids, and she noticed some of them trying to hide a smile. She knew what those looks and smiles meant: These kids were keeping a secret.

Time for her first experiment.

Looking over the class, Mrs. Marlow settled her eyes on Seth Townsend, smiled, and said, "So, Seth, did you do your science homework last night?"

With no hesitation, Seth smiled back and said, "Yes, I did."

Mrs. Marlow looked at Amy Gilson and said, "How about you, Amy?"

She nodded and said, "It was hard."

"Really? What did you think was hard about it?" she asked.

Amy scrunched up her face and then said, "Too much math."

Her answer got a lot of nods and a few laughs from the other kids, but then it went completely quiet again.

Mrs. Marlow couldn't get over how beautifully these children were behaving. Just yesterday, she had asked one student a question, and about fifteen others had blurted out answers, and then the whole class began arguing, and that had started a huge free-for-all that didn't end until she banged on her

desk with a book. It was always like that with this class, and with the other fifth-grade classes too.

But not today. No one talked at all . . . *unless* she asked a question.

Which gave Mrs. Marlow an idea.

"Please get out your homework sheets."

There was a lot of rustling and bustling as the students obeyed.

"Now," she said. "Ellen, look at problem number one. How did you decide if the given quantities were reasonable?"

Ellen riffled through her papers, and the look on her face surprised Mrs. Marlow: Ellen looked scared.

It was one of the standard questions about science problems, a question the whole class was used to. But the girl seemed completely confused. Mrs. Marlow could see that she'd done the assignment. Plus, Ellen was one of the best science students. What was she so scared about?

After a few moments of what looked like absolute panic, Ellen calmed down. Then, very slowly, she said, "The numbers . . . worked."

Mrs. Marlow waited for the rest of her explanation. It didn't come.

"Right," she said, "and . . ."

"I . . . made estimates," Ellen said.

Again, her words came slowly. And then there was another long pause.

"And . . . ," the teacher urged.

"I used . . . math."

Mrs. Marlow nodded. "Of course you used math. But I want to hear about your *process*, your *thinking*."

Ellen said, "I did . . . comparing."

Frustrated, Mrs. Marlow turned to the other side of the room. "Dave, tell us the answer you got for problem one. And explain your *process*."

Dave didn't look scared, but he also took a long time to respond—too long for Mrs. Marlow. She said, "I'd like your answer *today*, Mr. Packer."

Slowly, Dave said, "Four hundred forty."

" 'Four hundred forty' what?" prompted Mrs. Marlow.

"Barrels of oil," said Dave. Slowly.

"Per . . . ," said Mrs. Marlow.

Dave said, "Per . . . day."

"Wrong," said Mrs. Marlow. "Look at your work and tell me what you forgot." She was losing her patience.

Dave frowned and squinted at his paper. He nodded and then slowly said, "Um . . . the first day."

A ripple of giggles swept through the room—girl giggles.

Mrs. Marlow snapped, "Since when did wrong answers become funny?"

The science teacher thought, *Are they all pretending to be stupid today? Is that it?*

Whatever was going on, she didn't like it. It was disruptive. It was slowing down her class. It was annoying.

And suddenly Mrs. Marlow was in no mood for games. She was *not* going to play along. If these kids wanted quiet, then that's what they were going to get.

She glared around the room. "Pass in your papers."

Everyone obeyed without a word.

"Open to chapter four and read. The homework is on the board."

The next thirty-four minutes in the science room passed in complete silence, except for the rustle of paper and an occasional cough or sniffle.

And sitting at her desk, Mrs. Marlow had to admit that she enjoyed the quiet, enjoyed not having to fight the battle of the mouth every second with these kids. The Unshushables were completely shushed, all right—very weird.

But the science teacher wasn't any closer to figuring out *why* the kids were acting this way.

Dave felt something hit his arm and then drop onto his leg. It was a note.

He glanced at Mrs. Marlow. All clear. So he slowly reached down, picked up the note, and unfolded it.

> You said, "Um, the first day."
> _Um_ counts as a word.
> So you said four, and _you_ cost the boys one whole point—loser!
>   Ha-ha!
>   Lynsey

Dave knew Lynsey was sitting two seats back on his left. And he knew she was waiting for him to turn around so she could give him a sickly-sweet little smile.

So he didn't turn around. But he felt the tops of his ears getting pink. And he began thinking of a million things he wished he could say to her—all sorts of clever insults, like, _If brains were money, you'd be broke,_ or _Wow—you can count to four!_ or _I had a pet turtle that . . ._

"Mr. Packer—bring it here."

Dave snapped to attention and looked up to see Mrs. Marlow staring at him, holding out her hand.

Putting on his best innocent face, Dave said, "What?"

"The note. Here."

As Dave walked up and dropped the note into Mrs. Marlow's hand, the bell rang.

Mrs. Marlow tucked the paper into her pocket and then stood up quickly. Because when the bell rang, she had to hurry out her door and try to maintain law and order in the hallway between classes.

But, of course, there was no need for the corridor police, not today. Mrs. Marlow watched all the fifth graders move from room to room, smiling, waving, making faces, nodding at each other. There were a few laughs and whistles, and she heard Tyler Rennert make a loud snort in the general direction of some girls, but there was no talking.

She looked across the hall and caught Mrs. Escobar's eye, and they both smiled and then shrugged at each other. And since there wasn't any patrol work to do, Mrs. Marlow reached into her pocket and pulled out the captured note. And she read it.

For a logical person like Mrs. Marlow, Lynsey's note to Dave was like the Rosetta stone, a key that helped her begin to understand what she had seen and heard on the playground and then in her classroom.

So . . . this whole thing was something about counting words. More than three words resulted in a penalty—which explained all those short answers from Ellen and Dave. And it was the boys against the girls—nothing new about that, not with this group. And they were all trying to keep quiet.

Mrs. Marlow remembered the "jinx" game from her own school years, when two people said the same word at the same time and then had to keep quiet. Maybe it was like that.

Except this wasn't two people. It was more than a hundred and twenty-five of the most talkative children on planet Earth.

As chunks of the puzzle began to fall into place, Mrs. Marlow immediately thought, *The others are going to love this!*

She meant the other teachers.

But then her scientific curiosity kicked in, and she thought, *Why spoil the kids' experiment? And I should really let the other teachers figure things out on their own. And, of course, my preliminary findings could be wrong. I should certainly gather more data before I present my theory to the scholarly community.*

And as Mrs. Marlow chuckled at her private joke, she said to herself, *Kids!*

CHAPTER 12

GUESSING GAMES

Tuesday afternoon in the fifth-grade hall was a challenge for everyone.

Mrs. Akers walked into the music room, sat at her piano, smiled, and said, "My, you are all behaving so *well* this afternoon—wonderful! Now, please open your songbooks to 'This Land Is Your Land.'"

As she played the introduction on the piano, she said, "Backs straight, big smiles, deep breaths, and . . ."

No one sang.

The piano stopped mid-measure, and Mrs. Akers frowned at the class. "Now, I *know* you can all do better than that."

She began the introduction again, counting in the beats. "One, and two, and three, 'This land is your land, this land . . .'"

Mrs. Akers stopped. She was singing a solo, and

her high, quivering voice made the kids giggle.

She frowned again. "All right, students. This is *not* funny. And it's not good. We have less than two weeks before our Thanksgiving program, and we have no time for this kind of silliness."

She pointed a bright pink fingernail around the room. "Brian, Tommy, Anna, every one of you! I want to hear you *sing*!"

She banged out the introduction again, and the whole class sang, "This land is . . ." and then stopped.

The piano kept playing, and Mrs. Akers bellowed, "Sing!" And most of the kids jumped in on ". . . my land, from . . ." and then stopped.

After another shouted command, they sang ". . . the redwood forest . . . ," and that's how the whole song went, chopped up into three-word bits.

And when Mrs. Akers, her face bright red by this point, thumped on her piano and said, "What is *wrong* with all of you today?" the kids didn't say a word.

Like all teachers, Mrs. Akers understood the "divide and conquer" rule: When you need to get to the bottom of something, you don't ask the whole class; you ask *one* student. So she pointed at Lena in the front row and said, "Why aren't you singing?"

Lena hesitated, and then motioned at the kids all around the room and said, "Not talking today."

Mrs. Akers said, "What's that supposed to mean? Not talking?"

Lena nodded. "Only three words."

The music teacher was even more puzzled. She pointed at James and said, "Explain."

James had trouble expressing himself even under the best conditions. He gulped and took a deep breath. Then he said, "Not . . . words. Everyone."

A light dawned on Mrs. Akers's face. And, still talking to James, she said, "Oh—so, is it like that project kids do, when they take a vow of silence? To protest how there's still slavery in Africa? I read about that—is that it?"

James looked lost. He shook his head. "Hard . . . explain. Not."

But Mrs. Akers felt like she had answered the riddle, or maybe partly answered it. And whatever was happening, she decided to be a good sport.

Looking around the room, she said, "So, tell me—can you all hum? Is humming allowed?"

Everyone grinned and nodded like maniacs.

"How about clapping? Can you clap in rhythm?"

More smiles and nods.

"All right, then, here we go again," and she ripped back into the piano. "One, and two, and three! Hmm hmm hmm hmmm hmmm . . ."

And twenty-four fifth graders clapped and hummed along as Mrs. Akers played all seven verses of "This Land Is Your Land." Then the whole class giggled and laughed and hummed and clapped their way through the other four songs on the Thanksgiving program.

And they all survived their first wordless music class.

The fifth-period gym class was less dramatic than music. News had gotten to most of the teachers that the fifth graders had gone quiet, which didn't bother the gym teacher at all. Tuesday was dodgeball day, so Mrs. Henley appointed the two captains, and then the captains picked their teams by pointing, and the first game got under way—all without a word.

Dodgeball, which can be pretty serious anyway, seemed especially grim without the talking and shouting. There were the usual grunts of effort and screams of terror, and when three or four kids with red dodgeballs would silently go hunting for one player on the other team, it was sort of like watching a pack of wolves go after a lone caribou: A motion of the leader's head, a movement toward the prey, and then, *Whack! Whack! WHOMP!*—dead meat.

From the gym teacher's point of view, dodgeball was all about improving reflexes and getting a good large-motor-skills workout, and to accomplish those goals without any of the taunting and teasing and name-calling? That was just fine by her.

Even so, Mrs. Henley watched all three games with great interest, and she saw how the kids communicated without words. And she noticed herself pointing and shaking her head and blowing her whistle instead of yelling. It was nice to give her voice a rest.

Mr. Burton taught fifth-grade reading and language arts. He was puzzled at the beginning of the class right after lunch, and like the music teacher and the science teacher, he asked questions and got three-word answers. But he kept at it, and after about five minutes, he figured out what was going on, at least part of it.

Unlike Mrs. Marlow, Mr. Burton had a lot of patience and a pretty good sense of humor. And he couldn't see any real problem with having these kids be this well-behaved. Anything that got the Unshushables quiet was fine by him. Plus, he decided they could all have some fun with this limit of three words in a row.

He picked a funny story from their reading textbook, a really short one, and he had the kids read it out loud, three words each and as fast as possible, with him calling out the name of the next narrator.

And when the story was finished, he said, "Okay, now I want *you* to make up a story." He picked up a meter stick and said, "When I point at you, say a three-word sentence. And listen carefully, so you can make the story move forward. Here we go."

The story started like this:

"A woman screamed."

"She was scared."

"It was dark."

"'Oh, no—snakes!'"

"One bit her."

"'Ow! My leg!'"

"She limped outside."

"Her neighbor came."

"'What's wrong?'"

"'Snakes are everywhere!'"

"'Are they poisonous?'"

"'Yes, and smelly!'"

"'Quick, my car!'"

"'You saved me!'"

"'Darn! Dead battery!'"

Round and round the room the story went.

The poor woman and her neighbor were eventually eaten by the huge orange lizards that came up out of the sewers and ripped the roof off the car. The lizards also ate all the snakes. But then some ugly

tulips in the garden grew razor-blade teeth and ate the lizards. And then the tulips burped giant burps, which created a tornado that made the Statue of Liberty fall over and crush a tugboat, which made a wave that washed all the way to the White House and got muddy water all over the president's polka-dotted underpants.

It was quite a tale.

The period ended, and as the students walked quietly out of the room, Mr. Burton got a lot of waves and smiles and thumbs-ups. And he waved and smiled back at the kids. No words were needed.

It had been a successful class—fun, creative, lively, and everyone had used their word skills in new ways. Mr. Burton felt great.

The next forty minutes was his planning period, and then came the last class of the day, period seven. He had some papers to grade, but Mr. Burton was too excited. Because what these kids were doing— well, it felt like a once-in-a-lifetime chance to mess around with words and language and communica-tion, to try something fresh, something special. After all, science teachers aren't the only people who like a good experiment.

So Mr. Burton sat at his desk, thinking and think-ing. Finally, with about two minutes before period

seven, he got it—a great idea. Plus, he realized that this situation could be useful to him in a totally unexpected way.

And as the bell rang, Mr. Burton noticed that he was actually looking forward to his last class of the afternoon—another proof that this was *not* an ordinary day.

CHAPTER 13

LANGUAGE LAB

As his last class of the day came into Mr. Burton's room, he didn't speak, and of course, neither did the students.

The bell rang, and all the kids watched him as he put a stack of lined paper on the front desk of each row. Then he turned to the chalkboard and began to write.

Today there will be <u>writing only</u>. Nothing will be turned in, but everyone <u>must</u> write all period long, and everyone must communicate with at least four other people.

<u>You may not stop writing for more than fifteen seconds.</u>

As soon as you have paper, begin.

In less than one minute, every kid had paper. And in less than two minutes, the first notes were changing hands.

Todd wrote, "I still think this no talking thing is stupid," and he passed the paper to Kyle.

Kyle read the note and wrote, "I sorta like it. It's different. A challenge."

And then Todd wrote, "Challenge? What challenge? The teachers already know about it. Like Mr. Burton. He's just messing with us. Thinks it's great we're not talking. I LIKE TALKING!"

Kyle read, and he wrote back, "Too bad. Think how hard it is for all the blabby girls—we're gonna win this contest. Beat the girls! Beat the girls! Beat the girls! Get it? It's a silent cheer, like at a basketball game. Cool, huh?"

Todd wrote back, "Cool? Dude, it's lame. Here's my silent cheer—Kyle's a Dork! Kyle's a Dork! Kyle's a Dork!"

Kyle read the note, made a face at Todd, and then turned his back on him and started up a chat with Eric. No talking made it very simple to tune someone out.

A few seats away, Emily was having a hot argument with Taron. "I did not say you couldn't come over after school. I just said what's the point? If we can't talk. That's all."

Taron read the note, shook her head, and wrote, "I <u>know</u> you don't like me as much as you like Kelly. So stop pretending."

Emily rolled her eyes and wrote, "Don't be like that."

Taron shrugged and wrote, "Like what?"

Emily used block letters for emphasis. "ALL SNIFFY AND SNOOFY AND OUCHY—I <u>HATE</u> THAT."

"See?" Taron wrote. "<u>Hate</u>. That's what you said. You hate me."

Emily scribbled, "Don't be an idiot! I <u>don't</u> hate you. Come over after school. Really. We'll think of something to do. But we're gonna want to talk. I know we will. And we can't."

And Taron wrote back, "I'm NOT coming. <u>You</u> think I'm an <u>idiot</u>."

Emily read that, and then ripped the paper to pieces. And she reached across the aisle and patted Taron on the arm, and smiled her warmest smile, and then wrote on a fresh sheet of paper, "After school. My house, okay?"

Taron smiled back and nodded.

All around the room, kids were having to figure out the new rules for communicating. And for most of them, writing was a lot harder than talking. It was slower, like instant messaging—only less instant, and less fun because there was no computer to mess with. There was so much less give-and-take than there was with talking. The Unshushables weren't used to that. At all.

Dave had just finished a frustrating set of back-and-forth messages with Bill.

Bill couldn't understand how to keep from getting called offside during a soccer game. Dave had explained it three different ways. He had drawn pictures and diagrams and everything, and Bill still couldn't figure it out.

So Dave passed a note to Ed, because he was the best junior league player in town. "Bill doesn't get the offside rule. HELP!"

Ed read the note, nodded at Bill, bent over his paper, and began writing.

Dave looked around for a new partner, and he saw that Lynsey was passing notes with Helena. They seemed to be having a great time, nodding a lot and cracking each other up. *Probably gossiping,* he thought. *About something really stupid.*

He grabbed a clean sheet of paper and began a note to Lynsey: "What's the difference between you and a toxic waste dump?" But he decided that riddle was too harsh, even for Lynsey. Even if it *was* true.

He crumpled the paper and took another sheet.

But before he started writing, he got up, walked to a bookcase, and grabbed a dictionary.

He flipped the pages and then ran his fingers down a column of words. And there it was:

um also **umm** ([ə]m)
interjection. Used to express doubt or uncertainty or to fill a pause when hesitating in speaking.

So Lynsey had been right about something. For once.

He sat back down and wrote, "Hey, Captain Burgess, how's the war going? Ready to surrender?"

Dave nudged Jason, handed him the note, and pointed at Lynsey.

Jason nudged Lynsey and held the note out to her. And when she glared at him, Jason shook his head and pointed back at Dave.

Lynsey made a face and then took the paper, holding it between her thumb and forefinger like it was a squashed toad.

She read the message, wrote a little, and nudged Jason, who passed the paper back to Dave.

Her reply was, "It's <u>General</u> Burgess. Check the

score, dimbo. Girls rule, boys are losers. As usual. You're gonna get totally <u>schooled</u>!"

Jason handed the paper back to Dave. He read her message, made a snarly face at her, and then wrote, "Don't count on it. Always the big talker."

And sitting there frowning at the paper, once again Dave felt this overpowering wish that he could show Lynsey who was the boss, settle the question once and for all, really put her in her place.

And in answer to this wish, an idea popped into his head—an idea he probably should have ignored.

But he didn't.

Pressing down hard with his pencil, Dave wrote, "How about you and me go head-to-head, have our own special no-talking match? Starting right now, you and me. Unless you're scared. And the winner gets to write a big *L* on the loser's forehead. With permanent marker. On the playground after lunch on Thursday. How's <u>that</u> sound?" And he gave the paper to Jason.

Lynsey grabbed the paper from Jason and read it, and there was no hesitation. She looked at Dave, nodded a big yes, held up her hand with her fingers making an *L*, and pointed at him. Then she wrote something and handed the paper to Helena, who read everything, wrote something, and passed the paper back to Lynsey, who wrote something more and then passed the paper to Jason, who passed it back to Dave.

Lynsey had written, "Helena, you be the witness. Sign here." And Helena had written her name. And below Helena's signature, Lynsey had added, "No backing out now, fatmouth. Which color marker do you like best—red or black?"

Dave pointed at her and pretended to laugh and laugh. She stuck out her tongue and then turned away and picked up her chat with Helena.

Dave felt like he'd lost that skirmish. Lynsey always had a way of firing the last cannonball.

Then he smiled as he thought how much fun it would be to paint a big *L* on her forehead. If he could win, that is. Otherwise . . .

Dave wouldn't have put his feelings into these exact words, but he sat there in the quiet room sort of wishing it didn't have to be a war. Because it was . . . well, it was very *interesting*. Not talking was interesting all by itself, even without the extra fun of the contest. And the extra risk of his new private battle with Lynsey.

And he suddenly wondered what Lynsey thought about it, about the whole idea. And he wondered if she'd be honest enough to tell him.

So Dave grabbed a fresh sheet of paper and wrote, "I'm kinda glad we're all doing this—the no talking thing. Like, I really didn't know 'um' was a word. It's pretty interesting. At least it is to me." Then he gave the paper to Jason.

Jason tapped Lynsey's arm and handed her the new note. She read it and then gave Dave a short, suspicious look. And then she bent over the paper and wrote.

Jason handed him the paper, and Dave read her message. It said, "It is to me, too. I'm thinking and thinking and <u>thinking</u>. Pretty amazing."

Dave turned and caught Lynsey's eye, and they half nodded at each other. For one tiny fraction of a second, it wasn't boys against girls, and it wasn't a battle. It was two smart kids enjoying an idea.

Jason handed Dave another note, from him this time. "I'm <u>not</u> your personal delivery boy. Maybe you and Lynsey should sit at the same desk—ha ha ha!"

Dave's face felt hot. He scribbled "You're crazy!" onto Jason's note and jammed it back at him.

And at the bottom of the page he and Lynsey had passed, he wrote, "Yeah, but no way are you gonna win this fight. You and your stupid friends are going <u>down</u>, big-time!"

And as Dave tossed the note above Jason's head

so it landed on Lynsey's desk, he made an ugly face at her, and then shook his hands, like he was trying to flip something gross off his fingers.

He didn't wait for Lynsey's reaction. Dave turned away and began writing a new note. To Scott.

All during seventh period Mr. Burton sat at his desk, watching. He wrote some notes too, but they were notes to himself.

—No hesitation—everyone jumped right in.
—Some frustration with writing—it's slow.
—Some anger displayed.
—A lot of nodding and gesturing, some hand signals.
—Tapping on desks and arms and shoulders to get attention, some poking, too.
—Mouth sounds—tongue clicking, lip popping, raspberries.
—Some animal sounds—quacking, whistling, barking, sometimes to get attention, sometimes to bother.

−Not much boy−girl or girl−boy note passing−but more than I'd expected from this group.
−A lot of smiling and frowning and other face−making
−Not one single word out loud!

Mr. Burton was taking a class at the state university two nights a week, studying for his master's degree. The course was called Human Development, and one of the topics they had studied was the way children learn to use language.

Of course, this wasn't watching kids learn to *use* language. These students were already good with words. Almost too good.

No, this was watching children try to change how they expressed themselves, trying to use language in a new way.

Mr. Burton was pretty excited. It was like having his own private language lab. He thought, *If I keep careful notes, I bet I can write my big research paper on this! I can do interviews with the kids—once they start talking again. And I can gather information from the other teachers, too. There's so much good stuff to work with. This is great!*

When the last bell rang, Mr. Burton was sorry

the class had to end. And he couldn't wait for his first class on Wednesday morning.

For the fifth graders, that last bell on Tuesday meant something else.

It meant they had to go ride a bus. And not talk.

The bell meant they had to go to sports practice, or to dance or music lessons. And not talk.

It meant they had to go home and deal with moms and dads and brothers and sisters and neighbors and everyone else. And not talk.

No one was sure how all that was going to work, including Dave.

But Dave was absolutely sure of one thing: *He* was going to do everything just right. Because if he messed up, it meant he'd be walking around school on Thursday afternoon with a big *L* on his forehead.

And *that* was not going to happen.

CHAPTER 14

SEEN BUT NOT HEARD

The homebound school buses were quieter than usual on Tuesday afternoon, especially the ones hauling a large number of fifth-grade kids.

But none of the fifth graders found the ride home very hard. With no grown-ups around, it was pretty easy to keep quiet. A few of them sat with friends and passed notes back and forth. Some read books or opened a notebook and did homework. Most of the fifth graders just sat quietly—looking and listening. And thinking.

For the fifth graders like Lynsey who stayed for soccer or field hockey or cross-country, after school was just like regular school, because the coaches were all teachers, and you could answer teachers because of the three-word rule. Everyone was getting pretty good at that part of the contest.

Soccer practice was easy for Lynsey. Instead of yelling for the ball like she sometimes did, she just waved a hand or made a motion with her head. To direct teammates to cover an area or move down-field, she pointed. Lynsey was good at soccer. She did most of her communicating with her feet.

For the kids like Dave who went right home after school, not talking was more difficult. A *lot* more difficult. Because it's a fact of nature that parents don't like it when kids don't answer them.

"David?"

Dave had been home five minutes when he heard his mom come in the front door and call his name. He was upstairs. In the bathroom.

She called again. "David, answer me!"

To be more specific, Dave was sitting on the toilet.

"DAVID! ANSWER ME!"

Dave knew that tone of voice. He had to do something right away. So he reached over and banged on the inside of the bathroom door.

It was the wrong move.

His mom was up those front stairs and had both

hands on that locked bathroom doorknob in two seconds.

"David? Is that you? Are you all right? David? David! Answer me!"

She was going to kick down the door, Dave was sure of it.

He jiggled the doorknob, flushed the toilet, and was up and zipped and buttoned, all in about two seconds, and he yanked the door open and gave his mom the best smile he could manage.

Mrs. Packer was so relieved that she bent down and hugged Dave so hard that he couldn't have said a word even if he'd wanted to. Which he didn't.

But then she held him out in front of her and gave him a stern look. "Didn't you hear me calling you?"

It would have been easy to shake his head no and tell a silent lie, but Dave smiled and shrugged and held out his hands. Then he pointed at his mouth.

His mom frowned even more. "Your throat? Is your throat sore? Is that it?"

Dave shook his head.

"But it's hard to talk? Something hurts? Should I call Dr. O'Hara's office? We can drive right over there."

Dave shook his head again and motioned for his mom to follow him.

He went to his room, and then to his desk, and on a piece of paper he wrote, "Sorry. It's a thing we're doing at school. Not talking for a couple of days. That's all."

His mom looked at the paper. "Not talking?" she said. "Don't be silly. Everybody has to talk."

Dave smiled and shrugged. And he wrote, "Not <u>all</u> the time."

His mom tilted her head back and made a face at him, nodding slowly. "Ohhh . . . so you're saying that *I* talk all the time, is that it?"

Again, Dave smiled and shrugged.

"Because I could be as quiet as anybody." Then she added, "If I wanted to."

Bending over to pick up a sweatshirt, she pushed it into his arms and said, "Well, anyway, get the rest of these dirty clothes picked up and go downstairs and start a load in the washer. Only the dark colors, all right?"

Dave made a face, and she said, "And don't give me any of that sass, mister."

At his karate class Kyle did a front snap-kick— without a yell.

Mr. Hudson bowed and said, "Kyle-san. Always yell like this when you kick: Hii-*YAH*! Now you."

Kyle did the kick again, and he moved his face and mouth, but he didn't yell.

Mr. Hudson's face got red, and he walked stiffly like he always did when he was displeased. But he was still being polite, because that is the karate way.

He bowed. "Kyle-san. Did you not hear me?"

Ben Ellis walked onto the mat and bowed to Mr. Hudson. He was in fourth grade. When Mr. Hudson bowed back, Ben said, "Hudson-san. The fifth-grade kids aren't talking. None of them."

Hudson-san bowed and made a wise face and tried to imagine what the teacher in the movie *The Karate Kid* would say in this situation.

And after a long pause he said, "Ahh, I see. Yes. Silence. It is good."

Then he bowed at Kyle-san. And Kyle-san bowed back.

Then Kyle did another snap-kick. Without yelling.

Ellen played the first flute piece for her teacher, but there was a problem.

Mrs. Lenox said, "All right, we're in four/four time here." She used her pencil and pointed at a quarter rest. "How many beats of silence do you allow for this rest?"

Ellen tapped once on the music stand.

Her teacher said, "Correct, but just say, 'one beat.'"

Then Mrs. Lenox pointed at the symbol for a whole rest. "And how many beats for this one?"

Ellen tapped out four beats.

"Just say 'four beats,' dear."

Ellen smiled and tapped four times, and then pointed at her mouth and shook her head.

"What?" asked Mrs. Lenox.

Again Ellen pointed at her mouth and shook her head.

"Your lips? Something about your lips?" asked the teacher. "Just tell me, dear."

Ellen smiled and shook her head. Then she lifted the flute to her lips and played the piece again, and this time she read all the rests perfectly.

Her teacher nodded, smiled, and then turned the page to the next piece. Before Ellen began to play, Mrs. Lenox pointed at each rest, and Ellen tapped out the right number of beats. The teacher nodded, and Ellen began to play.

When she finished, Mrs. Lenox smiled, pointed at the start of the piece, picked up her own flute, nodded, and they played the whole piece again as a duet.

Neither of them said a word for the rest of the lesson.

•   •   •

Brian's mom picked him up at school, and when he got in the car, she said, "You need a haircut. We're stopping at Zeke's on the way home."

Brian groaned and shook his head. He stamped his feet on the floor of the car. His mom kept driving.

Brian hated going to Zeke's Modern Barbershop.

Zeke was this grumpy guy who'd been cutting hair in Laketon for more than forty years. He gave everyone the same haircut—short on top and buzzed close on the sides.

But the last two times he'd been there, Brian had forced Zeke to do a halfway decent job—but only because he practically yelled at the man the whole time. "Not so short on top. No, really, that's enough off the top. And don't use the clippers on the sides. Just scissors . . . there, that's enough. Don't cut off any more. Really. No, please, no clippers. Just use scissors. Please."

And that's why today was the wrong day for a haircut. If Zeke got him into that worn-out barber chair, Brian knew he'd end up looking like something that had escaped from the zoo.

When his mom parked the car, Brian jumped out and dashed into the pizza place next to the barber shop. But his mom followed him. He pointed at the menu, but she shook her head. "There's no time for a snack. We have to pick up your sister in fifteen minutes." She took him by the arm and pulled him out of the restaurant and over to Zeke's door. "Now get in there. Quick—there's no line right now."

Brian wanted to say, *News flash, Mom: There's never a line at Zeke's. The man's a rotten barber. And he has bad breath.*

But Brian couldn't say that. And he wouldn't be able to talk to Zeke, either. He was doomed.

Fifteen minutes later, when his big sister got into the car, she took one look at Brian and burst out laughing. She said, "Zeke, right?"

Brian could only nod. He had paid a heavy price for keeping his mouth shut. But he'd kept his promise to Dave and the other guys, and if they didn't beat the girls, well, it wasn't going to be his fault. And he had the bad haircut to prove it.

Was it worth it? *Yeah*, he thought, *it was worth it. So what if I look like a monkey for a week? Or two. Or three.*

Brian stared out the side window and tried not to think about it.

Mrs. Burgess was worried. She glanced in the rearview mirror and looked at her daughter's face again and thought, *Did she have a horrible day at school?*

Is that what's bothering her? Or maybe something happened at soccer practice—that coach of hers can be pretty rough.

About a month earlier, Lynsey had started riding in the backseat of the car instead of up front. Her mom had noticed that her bright, chatty little girl was starting to become more serious, sort of distant now and then. And today? Not even a word, and barely a nod as she got into the car after practice.

Lynsey's mom thought, *Maybe she's giving me the silent treatment because I said she couldn't go to that sleepover at Kelly's this weekend. That's probably it. Kids can be so moody sometimes—goodness knows I was!*

The truth is, Lynsey wasn't feeling moody at all. She was just thinking. Actually, she was thinking *about* thinking. Not talking all afternoon had made her realize something: For years now, she had done most of her thinking out loud. *I've been just blurting out whatever's on my mind—to my sister, to my mom—and at school? I just go on and on. And then I talk on the phone all night. Incredible!*

Lynsey hated to admit it, but Dave Packer might have been right about the top of her head exploding. Because that's how it had felt at first.

She felt like a faucet had been wide open, gushing and gushing forever, and then suddenly it flipped shut. And all her thoughts had been bottled up.

But by the time school let out, Lynsey had started to enjoy the change. And all during soccer practice, she'd felt like she was alone, just her and her own voice. And she'd felt like saying, *Hi there, I'm Lynsey—remember me? I live here.*

Thinking. And being quiet. It was different. And it was good.

As the car turned onto their street, almost home, she looked up and saw her mom's eyes in the car mirror, and instantly felt how worried she was. So Lynsey gave her mom a wave and a big smile. And her mom smiled back.

All over town, the other fifth graders were figuring out how to get along without talking. Were there any mistakes made on Tuesday afternoon? Yes, but only a few. Every single fifth-grade girl and boy was working hard not to talk.

And later on, as it got to be dinnertime and family time and homework time and bedtime, there were other problems the kids faced—a phone call from Grandma, a little brother who needed help with homework, a family trip to the mall for new shoes—lots of situations that begged for spoken words. Every single kid had unusual experiences Tuesday night, and every single kid had to be creative and alert . . . and quiet.

But it's not time to tell about all that.

It's time to go back to school, back in time to about three thirty on Tuesday afternoon, back to the conference room next to the office.

Because that's where the principal and the fifth-grade teachers had held a special meeting.

And they'd had *plenty* to talk about.

CHAPTER 15

CONTROL CENTER

"So. You've been with our fifth graders all afternoon. You've seen—and heard—what they're doing. What do you think should be done?"

Mrs. Hiatt looked from face to face around the conference table.

Mrs. Marlow spoke right up. "We should get them all in the auditorium tomorrow morning and lay down the law—just stop it. It's silly and it's disruptive. I mean, it's interesting, and all that. And with these kids, it's maybe even an improvement. But it's still not right. It was sort of cute right after lunch today, but then I had the second group, and then the third during seventh period. And by then it was just a bother, a real distraction. We've got a lot of material to cover in science. So I say we should squash the whole thing right away."

Mrs. Escobar nodded her agreement. "It's very

annoying in math class, these short answers they use. It's a game to them, and that's all they're paying attention to. I'm trying to work, and if they're playing a game, it's frustrating. Very frustrating. So if this is a vote, I say we stop it first thing tomorrow."

Mr. Burton shook his head. "But why? It's very inventive, what they're doing. And it's creative, and they're all thinking. And I think it's mostly positive, too. They're all exercising some self-control—which is a big change for this group. I think we should try to have a sense of humor about it, just let it run its course. It can't go on for very long, can it? What's the harm?"

"Well, it's not a problem in the gym," said Mrs. Henley. "Actually makes it easier, me not having to yell and all. I've got no complaints. If they want to be like they were this afternoon the whole rest of the year, it's perfectly fine by me."

"It's *not* fine by me." That was Mrs. Akers talking. "I only get them for music two or three times a week, and I need to make every minute count. And I asked Jim Torrey, and he feels the same way about art class. I went along with it this afternoon, and we had some fun, too. But I can't afford to waste more class time. I can't teach them songs if they won't sing more than three words in a row."

"I just realized something," said Mrs. Overby.

"You know what that little rascal Dave Packer did yesterday? Instead of giving an oral report, he stood up at the front of the class and coughed for two, maybe three whole minutes. And he was *pretending*, I'm sure of it. So he wouldn't have to talk! This really has to stop."

Mr. Burton said, "But don't you remember? We're talking about the Unshushables. These kids have been driving the whole school nuts for years and years. And suddenly, like some amazing gift from elementary school heaven, they all stop talking, and what are we going to do? We're going to start 'em right up again. That doesn't make sense. Why not wait a little? You know, see what happens. Just for another day or so. What's the harm in that?"

Mr. Burton honestly didn't think it was a problem. But even if he had, he would have asked the other teachers to back off anyway. He was hoping the quiet time would go on long enough for him to gather more information for that paper he needed to write for his Human Development class.

The principal had heard enough. She was glad to get everyone's opinion, but she didn't want the teachers turning against each other. This was *her* school, and like everything else, this decision was her responsibility.

Mrs. Hiatt said, "Thank you for your thoughts—very helpful. But this is not a voting situation. And I've made my decision. You know I've been trying to get these kids to quiet down ever since they were in first grade. So it's tempting to go along with this activity of theirs and hope it will lead to an improvement. But I think that would be wrong. The sudden quiet might seem easier than all the noise, but neither behavior is really what we want. These children need to learn to be quiet when it's right to be quiet, and they need to talk and participate at the right times too. We don't want an all-or-nothing situation—which is what this is. What we need is real balance, real self-control. If we let them keep up this game or contest or whatever it is, I think we'll be sending the wrong message. So we need to have an assembly tomorrow. I've noticed that Lynsey Burgess and Dave Packer seem to be the ringleaders. And I—"

"Actually," Mrs. Marlow interrupted, "I think it's more like Dave and Lynsey are sort of team captains. They're keeping score, counting words. And it's the boys against the girls. I intercepted a note."

The principal raised her eyebrows. "A note? You didn't tell me that."

Mrs. Marlow shrugged. "It was this afternoon. In my classroom."

Mrs. Hiatt said, "It might have been helpful if you'd told me about this sooner." The principal paused, letting everyone feel how displeased she was.

And in that moment, Mr. Burton thought, *Women—always keeping little secrets.*

But he immediately corrected that thought. Because anybody who hangs on to stereotypes about girls and boys . . . shouldn't. Especially if he's a teacher.

The principal said, "Anyway, that's good to know. And I think I see a way to approach the problem. So at the start of homeroom, please bring all the students to the auditorium."

It was quiet for a moment.

Then Mr. Burton said, "What are you going to do if the kids don't respond? To your approach."

Mrs. Hiatt looked at him, a trace of frost in her eyes. "What do you mean?"

"Well," he said, "I'm just saying that we've got five years of experience with this group. They've never obeyed very well when we've told them to stop being noisy. Why should it be any different when we tell them to stop being so quiet?"

Mrs. Hiatt stared at Mr. Burton a moment, and in her mind a little voice said, *Leave it to a man to say something negative.*

But, of course, she immediately corrected herself.

Because that kind of thought can get a principal in trouble. On a school faculty, it's never supposed to be girls against boys. In fact, that's called discrimination, which is against the law.

So Mrs. Hiatt looked around the table, smiled, and said, "All I can promise is that I'll do my best to resolve this situation in the most orderly way possible. And I know that each of you will do the same. See you all first thing in the morning."

As the teachers left the conference room, there wasn't much talking.

In fact, there was none.

CHAPTER 16

ORDERS

It was a bright November Wednesday, and the morning playground at Laketon Elementary School rang with the usual shouts and laughter of children.

But there was another layer of schoolyard activity going on—if a person knew what to look for. Because all around the swing sets and the jungle gym and the baseball diamonds, small groups formed up as fifth-grade friends passed notes and gestured and play-acted, trying to tell each other what had been happening since Tuesday after school; trying to tell each other all the clever ways they'd gotten along without talking. The fifth graders were so *glad* to see each other. They felt like they had spent Tuesday night in lonely prison cells, practically in solitary confinement.

There was also some contest business being

conducted. It was time for the first test of the overnight honor system. As agreed upon beforehand, boys who had spoken illegal words reported to Lynsey, and the girls reported to Dave.

As Dave received the morning confessions from a short line of sheepish girls, he felt pretty good. He added fifteen more points to the score against the girls.

Lynsey felt good too. By holding up fingers, four boys admitted that they'd spoken a total of twelve forbidden words—which seemed suspiciously low to her. But the rules were the rules, and she had to trust that the boys weren't lying—just like Dave had to trust the girls. And Lynsey admitted to herself that there might be a few cheaters on both sides. So it probably evened out. Anyway, she wasn't worried, because she was pretty sure that the girls were still winning.

When the first bell rang, everyone went inside.

Dave was in Mr. Burton's homeroom. When the second bell rang and all the kids sat silently at their desks, the teacher said, "Please line up at the door. We're going to a special fifth-grade assembly this morning. If anyone would like to guess what it's about, just speak up."

No one did, but Mr. Burton could tell from the

looks on their faces that most of them had a pretty good idea. He smiled and said, "But don't worry. Who could be upset with such beautifully behaved children? Not me, that's for sure."

After his group had filed into the auditorium and taken their seats, Dave turned and looked for Lynsey. She was sitting next to Kelly, and they were passing a note back and forth. She didn't look concerned at all.

Dave turned away quickly, so she wouldn't notice him looking at her. If Lynsey wasn't worried, he wasn't going to worry either—even though this assembly had to be about their contest. It *had* to be, didn't it? There had never been a special assembly at Laketon Elementary School before, at least not that he could remember.

And there had *certainly* never been an assembly that had begun in complete silence like this.

Lost in his thoughts, Dave didn't notice Mrs. Hiatt walking onto the stage. And she said something too, but he missed it.

Scott Vickers elbowed him in the ribs, and Dave snapped back to the present—just in time to see the principal looking right at him.

"Dave, I said I want you up here too."

In a daze, he looked around quickly and saw that Lynsey was already walking down the far aisle. So

Dave lurched to his feet, scooched past his class-mates, and hurried down the aisle and up the four steps onto the stage.

Mrs. Hiatt stood between them, and she said, "Now, as you know, students, we always begin an assembly with the Pledge of Allegiance. So, Lynsey, Dave, you will lead us in the Pledge this morning. Everyone, please stand up."

The whole fifth grade rose to their feet. In silence.

Dave glanced across at Lynsey, and she glanced at him. And the look they exchanged was clear: *What should we do?*

Lynsey gave a tiny shrug, and then they gave each other an even tinier nod. All of this happened in less than a second, and that's all it took for each to know that this was the right time for a temporary truce.

Dave and Lynsey looked out across the faces of their friends, nodded, put their right hands over their hearts, and turned to face the flag: signal sent, signal received.

These kids hadn't talked for more than eighteen hours. Every fifth grader took a deep breath, and if the pictures of Washington and Lincoln on either side of the stage had been painted with hands, they would have used those hands to cover their ears.

"I PLEDGE ALLEGIANCE TO THE FLAG
OF THE UNITED STATES OF AMERICA,
AND TO THE REPUBLIC
FOR WHICH IT STANDS,
ONE NATION, UNDER GOD, INDIVISIBLE,
WITH LIBERTY AND JUSTICE FOR ALL."

The kids spoke with one voice, almost shouting, incredibly loud, amazingly powerful—probably the most rousing Pledge of Allegiance ever heard in a public school during the entire history of the nation. The auditorium echoed, and it seemed to take a moment for the room to stop shaking.

As Dave and Lynsey hurried back to their seats, Mrs. Hiatt, her ears still ringing, said, "Thank you. That was . . . excellent. I have called this special fifth-grade assembly so that every one of you gets the same message at the same time. As of right *now*"—and here, the principal paused and swept her eyes over the upturned faces in front of her—"the contest, or game, or whatever you'd like to call this sudden quietness, or this three-words-in-a-row business you're all doing—as of right now, it's *over*. Ended. Stopped. It was interesting, and I hope you learned something, and we all hope that you also enjoyed yourselves. But I have decided that it needs

to stop. What you've been doing has made it very difficult to have normal, productive classroom activities. And, of course, that is why we're all here, to learn as much as we can every day. So, is that clear?"

The room was silent, and then a scattering of kids replied, "Yes, Mrs. Hiatt."

The principal said, "Is what I am saying clear to *everyone*?"

This time the whole group responded, "Yes, Mrs. Hiatt."

But there was no sudden rush of whispering, no undercurrent of talking in the auditorium, no joking and laughing—none of the usual behavior that the Unshushables were famous for.

The group remained silent.

And Mrs. Hiatt realized something: Yes, the kids had all responded to her, and just now they had all obediently said, "Yes, Mrs. Hiatt." But—that was only *three* words. And now it was still completely silent in the auditorium.

So, to really prove that they had actually *agreed* to behave normally, well . . . she would have to get them all to start talking . . . normally.

But the principal instantly decided that this did not feel like the right moment to push it. Better to let the teachers work it out with smaller groups, one class at a time.

So she smiled at the fifth graders and said, "Thank you for listening so carefully, and now I hope you all have a wonderful day. Teachers, you may take your first-period classes now."

Mrs. Hiatt watched the classes leave, one by one. It was a very orderly exit. All the kids were behaving extremely well.

But it didn't feel right. It was just too quiet.

CHAPTER 17

ALLIANCES

As he walked toward his first period class, Dave felt relieved. He was glad Mrs. Hiatt had put an end to the contest. He was especially glad that he wouldn't have to actually mark a big *L* on Lynsey's forehead. Or the reverse of that. Now he could just think about his schoolwork again. Because he really was a pretty good student. That's why he was in the high math group.

But as he went into the math room, he didn't talk to his friends, and they didn't talk to him. And none of the girls were talking either. No one was actually sure that the contest was over. And no one was taking chances. Including Dave.

The bell rang, and as everyone took their seats it was still completely quiet.

Mrs. Escobar got right down to business. "All right, students, we're still working on metric conversions, and, let's see . . . who's got an answer for the first home-work problem?"

Lynsey raised her hand, and when Mrs. Escobar nodded, she said, "Three hundred twelve."

Mrs. Escobar frowned. " 'Three hundred twelve' what?"

Lynsey said, "Degrees Celsius."

Mrs. Escobar looked at Lynsey. "You heard what the principal said a few minutes ago?"

Lynsey nodded.

"About how this little game needs to stop?"

Lynsey nodded again, and then raised her hand.

Mrs. Escobar nodded, and Lynsey said, "But why?"

"Why?" said the teacher. "Because it's not good. For anyone. It slows down our classwork. Like right now. We should be doing math, and instead we're talking about . . . not talking."

Lynsey said, "Math is numbers."

"Yes," said Mrs. Escobar, "but we need to use words to talk about how we're using numbers. You know that. You all know that. So stop this. Right now."

Lynsey stood up and pointed at the dry erase board. "May I?"

Mrs. Escobar said, "Go ahead."

Lynsey had her homework paper in one hand and a marker in the other. She wrote out the numbers for the first problem and then showed the three steps she used to get the correct answer.

She turned to Mrs. Escobar, and when the teacher nodded, she said, "How's that?"

Mrs. Escobar was starting to boil over. "I am *not* amused by this, Lynsey. I know what you're doing, and I will *not* stand for it. Now *stop it!*"

Lynsey stood at the board. She pointed at the problem. "Is it right?"

Another three words.

Dave knew that look on the teacher's face. It meant trouble, serious trouble. And not just for Lynsey. He held his breath, waiting for the explosion.

But the very next moment, Dave amazed himself: He raised his hand.

Mrs. Escobar had to grit her teeth, but she managed to say, "Yes?"

Dave pointed at the solution on the board and said, "Mine is different."

Without asking permission, Dave was on his feet. He grabbed the marker from Lynsey and scrawled his work onto the board. He had the same answer, but he had worked with fractions instead of decimals.

Mrs. Escobar said, "How many of you did it the way Dave did?"

About half the hands went up.

"And the way Lynsey solved it?" The other half went up.

The teacher nodded. "That's good. Does everyone see why it can be done both ways?"

Everyone nodded.

"Okay, here's a tougher question: Kelly, which way was easier, Dave's way or Lynsey's way?"

Kelly said, "Lynsey's."

"Really?" asked the teacher. "How come?"

"Fewer steps."

And all around the room, Mrs. Escobar saw heads nodding, saw the special light that shows up on a kid's face when understanding happens.

She smiled. "That's right. Decimals really do make things easier."

Tyler raised his hand and said, "With a calculator." Which got a laugh from the whole class.

And as they laughed, Dave and Lynsey looked at each other for about half a second. Not quite a friendly look, but similar.

Then Dave thought, *This means the contest is still on.* And he wasn't sure how he felt about that.

The class sailed through the rest of the conversion

problems—miles to kilometers, kilograms to ounces, acres to hectares, on and on. And every student responded using three words or less, or with written answers on the board.

Mrs. Escobar knew the kids weren't obeying Mrs. Hiatt. She knew they were still counting words, still keeping silent unless called on.

But honestly, at this moment, she didn't care. She was in the middle of an amazingly productive class period—and everyone was so focused, so alert, so engaged. Compared to the classroom experience she'd had with these same kids just twenty-four hours ago, well, it was like night and day. And she liked the day much better.

And what was happening in the other first-period classrooms on Wednesday—classrooms where Lynsey and Dave were not on hand to provide some leadership?

As science class began, Mrs. Marlow had already decided to make an example of the first kid who gave her a three-word answer. And it happened to be Kyle.

"I *asked* you to tell me about the order Lepidoptera," the teacher said.

Kyle nodded. "Butterflies and moths," he repeated.

"And that's all you know?" she said.

He nodded again. "Pretty much." Which got a giggle from the class.

Mrs. Marlow grabbed a notepad and picked up a pencil, reading out loud as she wrote: "Dear Mrs. Hiatt, Kyle has refused to obey your instructions. He is not participating in class discussion, and he—"

Kyle raised his hand, and Mrs. Marlow snapped, "What?"

"I'm participating."

"No," she said, "you're *deliberately* using as few words as possible, and you are disobeying the principal."

Kyle shook his head. "I'm . . . conserving."

She said, "That's nonsense. Conservation means . . ."

Kyle finished the sentence: ". . . not wasting."

Mrs. Marlow glared at him. "Conservation is for energy and water and soil and forests. Words don't need conserving."

"Maybe they do," Kyle said, which was awfully brave of him.

And all the kids in the class nodded their agreement with Kyle. Which was also very brave.

Mrs. Marlow felt herself getting angry. However, she was an extremely logical person, and she had to admit that Kyle had a point. Anybody who had ever eaten lunch in the teachers' room or sat through a whole faculty meeting would have to agree that a *lot* of words get wasted every school day. And all that endless gabbing that had made the Unshushables so famous? Ninety-nine percent waste.

But she said, "Regardless of that, the principal said you must all participate *normally* in class."

Kyle scrunched up his face. "What's normal?"

Mrs. Marlow said, "In this case, it means talking the way the principal wants you to . . . the way I want you to . . . the way everyone usually talks and answers . . . normally."

Kyle said, "Can normal change?"

"Well . . . ," and Mrs. Marlow paused.

She paused because just three days ago they had discussed climate change, and she had explained how a normal high temperature *now* would have been considered *abnormal* a hundred years ago. And she knew Kyle would remember that. The whole class probably remembered. This was a very bright group.

She continued. "Yes, you could say that. But it's certainly not normal to use only three words at a time. Or no words at all. Not at school."

Kyle shrugged. "Works for me."

Mrs. Marlow thought back to all the times in the past week when she'd had to yell at Kyle about his nonstop whispering, about his constant joke-telling, about his never-ending comments on anything and everything that ran through his twitchy little head. And she looked at Kyle sitting there quietly, giving her his full attention. And every other student was doing the same thing.

And suddenly, the idea of trying to *make* these kids talk, actually *demanding* that they all go back to being noisy, self-absorbed chatterbrains—it simply wasn't . . . logical.

So Mrs. Marlow decided to go ahead with her lesson for the day, and she adjusted herself to the new normal. Because the *new* normal was at least ten times better than the *old* normal.

In social studies there were more oral reports, and Mrs. Overby called on Ed Kanner and Bill Harkness to go first.

The boys walked to the front of the room, stood shoulder to shoulder, and both of them looked down at the index cards in Bill's hands.

Ed said, "Italy is old."

Then Bill said, "The Roman Empire . . ."

And Ed said, "Ruled the world . . ."

And Bill said, "For many centuries."

And Mrs. Overby said, "*What* do you two boys think you're doing?"

Ed said, "Giving our report."

And Bill said, "On Italy."

"No," said the teacher, "you're still playing that game, counting the words."

"But we practiced," Ed said.

"We're ready," Bill said.

And Ed said, "Can we finish?"

Like the other teachers up and down the fifth-grade hall, Mrs. Overby had to make a decision: Go with the flow—which promised to be very quiet and orderly—or call for the principal, raise a ruckus, and try to force these kids to be their regular old noisy selves again.

As a student of history, Mrs. Overby knew about the power of a grassroots movement. She also knew about the power of civil disobedience.

But mostly, she decided that this no-talking craze was actually a pretty good social experiment. Plus, she didn't feel like the kids thought they were winning and she was losing—it wasn't like that. They were just having a different kind of communication experience—together. That's all.

True, Ed and Bill's report on Italy was choppy

and awkward and a little hard to follow as they passed the narration back and forth like a Ping-Pong ball. But the boys made all their points, learning took place, and the whole class sat silently and paid close attention. And the next five reports went almost as smoothly. What more could a social studies teacher ask for?

So, like the other teachers, Mrs. Overby chose the quiet way.

And she decided she'd talk to the other teachers later in the morning and see how they were handling this thing. And she'd talk to Mrs. Hiatt, too.

Language arts was the easiest class for the kids. Mr. Burton didn't even try to make them stop their "activity." If they wanted to be quiet and talk only in three-word bursts, he was all for it, no matter what the mighty Mrs. Hiatt had said. After all, this was his classroom, wasn't it? And if he believed this way of using words could provide a good language arts learning experience, then couldn't he proceed with it? Yes. Absolutely.

But he wasn't foolish. He walked to the back of the room, stuck his head out into the hallway, looked both ways, and then closed his door.

Back at the front of his room, Mr. Burton said,

"Eric and Rachel, please come up and sit in these chairs."

When they were seated, he said, "You two are going to have a short debate. A debate is an orderly argument, and each of you will take opposite sides on the same issue. And the question is, 'Should there be soft-drink machines in school cafeterias?' Rachel, you will argue *for* this question, and Eric, you will argue *against* it. You will take turns speaking . . . *and* you may use no more than three words for each statement. Ready?"

Eric and Rachel shook their heads no.

Mr. Burton said, "Don't worry. You'll both do fine. Eric, you first. And, you may begin."

Eric said, "Soft drinks . . . bad."

Rachel shook her head and said, "Not bad. Delicious."

Eric frowned. "Too much sugar."

Rachel said, "I like sugar."

Eric shook his head. "Sugar rots teeth."

Rachel smiled a big smile. "Not mine."

Eric said, "Milk is better."

Rachel shrugged. "Try sugar-free."

Eric said, "Still, bad . . . nutrition."

Rachel held up her arm and made a muscle. "I eat vegetables."

Eric said, "Not everyone does."

Rachel said, "I like choosing."

Eric said, "Soda is . . . expensive."

Rachel pulled a dollar from her pocket. "I have enough."

Eric said, "Spend it smarter."

Rachel said, "What about freedom?"

Eric shook his head. "Not at school."

Rachel smirked. "Very bad news!"

And they went on like that for about five minutes with no letup.

All the kids were fascinated, and, of course, so was Mr. Burton.

He took furious notes, writing down each response, trying to record the kind of gestures the kids made, their facial expressions, their tones of voice.

Very few words were being exchanged, but whole worlds of ideas were floating around as the kids tried to build their arguments. They got emotional, and the three-word limit was clearly a problem. Still, they packed a lot into so few words. It was like debating with condensed haiku.

It was also sort of like listening to cave people talk, or maybe Tarzan—"Hungry, eat now." And Mr. Burton wrote some three-word chunks of his own, which he intended to use in his Human Development paper:

-*Every word counts.*
-*Choose power words.*
-*Hemingway would approve.*
-*Focus and narrow.*
-*Ideas are collapsible.*
-*Remember Miles Davis.*

And as he looked at what he wrote, he thought, *Maybe I should write my whole paper using three-word sentences. That would certainly get the attention of my professor!*

In music class, the kids entered the room and sat silently, just like yesterday afternoon. Mrs. Akers was sure the students were going to disobey Mrs. Hiatt's orders, and she was ready to take some drastic steps to stop this nonsense.

But· when she played an introduction and launched into "Over the River and Through the Woods," everyone sang right out.

The teacher was amazed. Mrs. Akers felt like there had been a glorious victory for the forces of law and authority, and she intended to write the principal a special note to say thanks for her strong leadership.

In fact, though, the principal's talk was *not* the direct cause of the singing.

Taron had written a simple note, and she'd shown it to all the boys and girls as they came into the music room:

Singing is <u>not</u> talking. Deal?

And by nodding, all the boys and all the girls had silently agreed that bending the contest rules a little was a good idea. Besides, no one wanted the Thanksgiving music program to sound lousy, and their contest would be over by then, anyway.

The boys and girls in that first-period music class might not have noticed it, but the important thing was not that they had agreed to sing. The important thing was that they had *agreed*. About anything. Fifth-grade boys and fifth-grade girls at Laketon Elementary School were actually cooperating and helping each other.

And that's what was happening in the other fifth-grade classrooms too. The boys and girls had joined forces without even realizing it. Together, they had resisted the pressure from the principal and from their teachers. They had used their wits and teamed up to prove that not talking was a simple, harmless activity. It wasn't like the boys and girls were getting all buddy-buddy or anything, and it wasn't like the teasing and taunting had completely stopped. Because old habits are hard to break.

But still, cooties were dying all over the place.

That was one result.

Another result of the morning classes was that the kids had won a new kind of respect from their teachers. Teachers have great respect for order and self-discipline. Teachers love to make careful plans and then put them into action—it's what they do. And teachers hate noise and disorder and bouncing kids, because these things keep them from accomplishing their careful plans.

However, there was one gigantic problem with all this harmony and order and balance and peace that was blooming in the fifth-grade hall: Mrs. Hiatt wasn't in the loop. She was clueless about these new developments.

In fact, the principal wasn't even in the building during the morning. She was across town at the district offices working on next year's budget. She had left her trusty teachers to carry out her strict orders.

But Mrs. Hiatt had organized her meetings to be sure that she would be back at her school in time for fifth-grade lunch. Because the principal felt sure she would be needed at lunch. With her bullhorn. To keep law and order, just like always.

Because Mrs. Hiatt had complete confidence in her teachers.

She was sure that by lunchtime everything would be back to . . . normal.

CHAPTER 18

ADVENTURES IN THE RED ZONE

Mrs. Hiatt got back to her school at 11:59. There were several messages on her desk, and Mrs. Overby had taped a note on her chair that read, "Please come see me in the teachers' room."

But the principal was in a hurry. She needed to be on time for fifth-grade lunch.

Five minutes later, for the second day in a row, Mrs. Hiatt found herself standing in the middle of a silent cafeteria holding a big red plastic bullhorn.

But today, it was different.

She looked around the quiet room, and the sight of all these fifth graders *deliberately* disobeying her— well, it nudged her over the edge. It pushed her right into the red zone.

She gritted her teeth, and an angry haze filled her mind, and she knew she was angry, and she knew it wasn't good to be angry. But she was.

And she knew it wasn't good to be angry and try to talk to children at the same time.

But she couldn't help herself. She *had* to talk to these kids. Right now.

She could have whispered, and every fifth grader would have heard her. But she didn't whisper.

She pulled the trigger on the bullhorn.

"HAVE YOU FORGOTTEN OUR ASSEMBLY THIS MORNING?"

The principal's voice echoed off the walls.

The kids stared at her.

She aimed the bullhorn at Dave and yelled, **"DAVID PACKER, ANSWER ME: DO YOU REMEMBER WHAT I TOLD ALL OF YOU THIS MORNING?"**

When Dave nodded his head, she yelled, ***"ANSWER* ME. WITH YOUR *VOICE*. OUT LOUD."**

So Dave swallowed his first bite of macaroni and cheese and said, "I remember." His voice sounded very small. Dave felt like he was the Scarecrow talking to the Great and Powerful Oz.

Mrs. Hiatt took five steps closer to Dave and

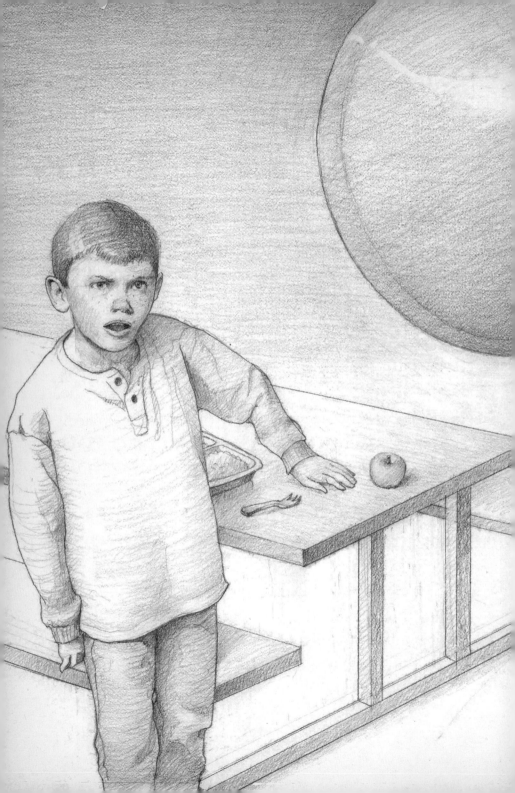

shouted, **"THEN WHY AREN'T YOU TALK-ING WITH YOUR FRIENDS?"**

Dave had never seen Mrs. Hiatt this mad before. And no one had ever yelled at him with a bullhorn. It seemed unfair. To be yelled at with that giant voice. So he decided he wasn't going to be afraid. Or angry. No matter what.

Dave shrugged and said, "Nothing to say."

Which was perfectly true. Before Mrs. Hiatt had started yelling, he had been very happy to just sit and eat and think.

"STAND UP!"

Dave stood up. Every kid in the room was watching him. And so was Mrs. Marlow. And the custodian. And the cafeteria workers.

Mrs. Hiatt said, **"TALK. I WANT YOU TO TALK RIGHT NOW. I WANT TO HEAR YOU TELL TODD EVERYTHING YOU LEARNED IN ALL YOUR CLASSES THIS MORNING. START TALKING TO TODD. NOW."**

Dave wasn't an angry sort of kid. Not usually.

In fact, there was only one thing that nudged him over the edge: being bullied. The only time he'd ever gotten into a fight at school was back in second grade when a fifth grader had started picking on him. That's when Dave had learned that you can't just go along with a bully. Because then you get bullied more and more.

And that's how Dave felt. Right now. He was getting mad. It felt like Mrs. Hiatt was being a bully—a bully with a bullhorn.

Again the principal yelled, **"TALK!"**

And that did it. It was Dave's turn for a trip to the red zone.

He glared at Mrs. Hiatt, and he shouted, "I do *not* have to talk now if I don't want to. This is *our* lunch time. *None* of us have to talk!"

And a sentence flashed into Dave's mind, something he had heard dozens of times on TV shows. This sentence was usually being said to criminals wearing handcuffs, but that didn't seem to matter at the moment.

Dave looked around the cafeteria at his classmates, and he shouted, *"You have the right to remain silent!"*

And with that, Dave pressed his lips together, folded his arms across his chest, and sat down.

Lynsey was the first to pick up on Dave's body language. She looked at Mrs. Hiatt and slowly folded her arms. All the girls at her lunch table did the same.

And the gesture spread through the room like

ripples on a pond. Every kid stared at the principal, arms folded and stone silent.

Mrs. Hiatt looked around slowly, drew herself up to her full height, and then walked briskly out of the room. She walked down the hall to the school office. She nodded at Mrs. Chaplin, the school secretary, and said, "Hold my calls." Then she went into her own office and closed the door.

Back in the cafeteria, it was dead calm. Every kid sat motionless, arms still folded, not sure what to do next.

Todd started it.

He unfolded his arms and nodded at Dave, and then he clapped his hands. In three seconds every fifth-grade boy was clapping like mad.

Dave looked around at his friends and smiled and nodded.

And a second later, guess who joined in? That's right: all the girls.

And five seconds later, the hooting and the whooping began.

It was loud in that cafeteria. It was *incredibly* loud.

The clapping and cheering was so loud that the sound went right through the cafeteria doors and walls and thundered down the hall—all the way to the school office, and right through the closed door of Mrs. Abigail Hiatt, principal.

The phone on Mrs. Chaplin's desk buzzed—an intercom call.

"Yes?" she answered. The secretary listened, nodded, and said, "Right away."

She got up and walked out of the office and down the hall and into the cafeteria, where it had gotten quiet again.

Mrs. Marlow was standing near the doorway, and Mrs. Chaplin whispered something to her.

Mrs. Marlow nodded and quickly walked halfway across the room.

She bent down close to Dave Packer's ear and said, "To the office."

Dave swallowed his third bite of macaroni and cheese and looked up into the science teacher's face. "I have to?"

She nodded, "Principal's orders."

Dave looked around the table at his friends. No one needed to speak a word—their faces said it all. And the message?

Three simple words, and Dave believed them: "You are *dead*!"

CHAPTER 19

APOLOGIES

There were two hundred and twenty-seven green tile squares on the hallway floor between the cafeteria and the school office. Dave counted each one to keep from thinking about what was going to happen next. But he thought about it anyway.

Mrs. Chaplin pointed at the principal's door. "Go right in."

Dave knocked. He knew he didn't have to, but it bought him another two seconds of delay.

Mrs. Hiatt said, "Come in," and Dave thought, *At least she's not using her bullhorn.*

He opened the door, and she was standing with her back to him, looking out the windows into the school courtyard.

Dave blurted out, "I'm sorry," and he said that because he knew he shouldn't have yelled at the

principal, even if he had been right. Which he still believed he was. He also apologized because he hoped it might help save his life.

Mrs. Hiatt turned around, and Dave was shocked to see the look on her face. Because she wasn't mad. She almost looked like she'd been crying, and her nose was pink.

She shook her head. "That's why I sent for you, so *I* could say that. I'm the one who got angry. And I yelled first, and I set a terrible example. So I hope *you'll forgive me.*"

Dave couldn't remember the last time a grown-up had apologized to him. And to have the *principal* saying she was sorry, well, he could barely manage a nod at her.

She nodded back, and then paused and said, "So, what are we going to do about this . . . situation?"

"Um . . . not sure," Dave said.

She frowned. "Please, you can talk freely in here. None of your friends can hear us."

Dave shook his head. "Honor system."

Mrs. Hiatt's eyebrows went up. "Oh? Of course. Very admirable. Well, maybe you can answer some questions for me, just to get started."

Dave said, "Sure."

"First of all, how did all this get going? Who started it?"

Dave smiled. "Mahatma Gandhi."

"Pardon me?" Mrs. Hiatt said.

Dave said, "He stopped talking."

The principal said, "And someone wanted to try that here, at school, right?"

Dave nodded, and pointed at himself. "All my fault."

"I see," she said. "How did you learn about Gandhi?"

He said, "Social studies report."

"And why did he stop talking?"

Dave shrugged. "To think more."

"But you're not keeping *silent*, not totally—why?"

Dave thought a moment and then said, "Respect. For school," which he knew was going to make him sound like a goody-goody. But it was true. He and his friends weren't trying to shut down the school. Not at all.

Mrs. Hiatt nodded slowly and said, "Oh."

She seemed to be out of questions.

And during that three or four seconds of silence, an idea jumped into Dave's mind—but he pushed it out. It was too outrageous.

But the idea bounced back into his head, and this

time Dave just blurted it out. "Want to join?"

Mrs. Hiatt bunched her eyebrows together. "What do you mean?"

"Join—stop talking."

She looked at Dave as if he had just told her to put on a grass skirt and dance the hula on the roof of a school bus. "Don't be silly—I'm the *principal*. Do you have any idea how many people I have to speak to? Every single day?"

Dave pointed at a notepad on her desk.

"May I?"

She nodded, and he wrote, "You can say only three words in a row. And only if a teacher or a grown-up talks to you first. Except you can talk to a kid first. Because you're sort of a teacher. And no talking at all outside of school—honor system. And the whole thing's almost over anyway—just until tomorrow."

Then Dave smiled up at her and said, "It's . . . interesting."

Mrs. Hiatt shook her head. "I could never—"

Dave put up his hand like a traffic officer: "There! Stop: three."

Mrs. Hiatt smiled—and it wasn't a principal smile. Dave could tell. She was smiling a real person smile.

She smiled because she realized Dave had offered her something important. Just five minutes earlier she had acted like—like a monster. But she wasn't, not really.

Still, she *had* behaved terribly. Everyone in the cafeteria knew that, kids and grown-ups both. And news like that spreads quickly. So somehow she needed to remind everyone that she *wasn't* a monster—fast.

And Dave had just offered her a way to become human again. Because it's a well-known fact that monsters do *not* have a sense of humor.

She tore Dave's sheet off the notepad, bent over the desk, and did some writing of her own.

She stepped quickly into the office and handed Mrs. Chaplin the paper.

The secretary read it over quickly and said, "And I should . . ."

The principal held up one finger and said, "Type." Then she held up two fingers and said, "Duplicate." And then she held up three fingers and said, "Distribute."

And Mrs. Chaplin said, "Got it."

Then, turning to Dave, the principal said, "Ready, set, go."

Dave's head was spinning, but he managed to say, "Where?"

She was already out the office door, and over her shoulder Mrs. Hiatt said, "To the cafeteria."

CHAPTER 20

THE WINNERS

At this point, it might be fun to tell how Dave followed the principal back to the cafeteria, and how Mrs. Hiatt apologized to the whole fifth grade—by trading three-word phrases back and forth with Dave. Who also apologized.

And describing the looks on the faces of all those fifth graders in the cafeteria, not to mention Mrs. Marlow and the rest of the staff—that might be fun too.

Or it might be interesting to tell how Mrs. Hiatt called an all-school assembly five minutes later by chiming the school intercom and then saying, "Everyone: auditorium. Hurry!" And how all the teachers in every grade were given five minutes at the assembly to explain the new no-talking rules to their students, and how loud and confusing it was as they did that; and then how completely quiet it got when the principal announced, "Silence starts . . . NOW!"

And it might be enlightening to explain how Mrs. Hiatt had changed the contest, so that the kids in kindergarten through fourth were competing grade against grade to see who could say the fewest illegal words during the next twenty-three hours— and why she thought her way was a better idea than boys against girls.

And it might be thought-provoking to explain how Dave felt about all this—how he felt that he was sort of like Gandhi, and how Mrs. Hiatt was sort of like the British Empire, and how he felt like there had been a great victory, "with liberty and justice for all"—which included Mrs. Hiatt herself.

And Mr. Burton—there's a lot that could be told about him, because he went completely stratospheric. He spent the last twenty-four hours of the contest scribbling down notes, taking photos, and using a little handheld recorder to capture as many three-word sentences as possible. He collected so much great material that he began thinking that he could not only write that paper for his Human Development course, he could practically write a whole *book* about the way the kids and teachers at Laketon Elementary School had changed the way they expressed themselves, changed their view of language itself—what it is, and how it works, and how communication can take so many different forms.

And speaking of human development, it might be fun to explore why the very youngest kids could not even *imagine* how to go without something as amazing and powerful as talking, not even for ten minutes—which is why the whole kindergarten was immediately excused from the activity.

And how about Thursday morning—when the boys reported zero honor system word-goofs and the girls reported only one? Telling how Dave and Lynsey reacted to *that* news would be revealing.

And then it would certainly be fun to peek at the challenges Mrs. Hiatt faced as she kept to a strict diet of three words at a time. On Wednesday afternoon, and again on Thursday morning, she talked with parents, with the superintendent, with the principals of other schools, with the electrician who arrived to repair the milk cooler, and, of course, with her teachers and with hundreds of kids—all of whom thought it was great to have a principal who just might be a little bit crazy.

In fact, the story could jump a whole week ahead, or even months ahead to see the way the fifth graders completed the school year as kinder, more careful talkers. And thinkers.

Because there's absolutely more to tell. There's *always* more.

But, as tempting as it is, it's not the time to tell about all that. Because this is the time to jump right to fifth-grade lunch on Thursday, right to that point when the *original* contest was coming to an end, right to that moment of truth when the boys and the girls were getting ready to compare their final scores.

Because with all the goodwill and the happy vibes that swirled out of Mrs. Hiatt's change of heart, plus the excitement of having the whole school go quiet, you might think that somehow the fifth-grade boys-against-girls contest didn't matter anymore.

But it did.

Remember when Dave stood up and shouted at the principal on Wednesday? Did you think no one was counting? Not true: *Everyone* was counting. Dave had said thirty words—grand words, brave and true. *However* . . . all but three of them were illegal.

At 12:14, one minute before the end of the contest, the cafeteria was silent. Every fifth grader was watching the second hand on the big clock. And so were all the fifth-grade teachers. And Mrs. Hiatt. And the custodian. And the school secretary, and the school nurse, too. No one wanted to miss this moment in the history of the Unshushables.

Dave and Lynsey sat across from each other at the same lunch table, ready for the big tally. Dave dug around in his back pocket and found the crumpled sheet listing all the points against the girls. And Lynsey pulled her little red notebook and a pencil out of her backpack, and she bent over it, adding and scribbling away.

Glancing down, Dave saw something poking out of the top pouch of Lynsey's backpack: a huge permanent marker, a red one.

And Dave had no trouble at all imagining a big *L* on his forehead. Because he already knew the final scores for both teams, and he was sure Lynsey did too.

With just fifteen seconds to go in the silent cafeteria, Lynsey stood up, looked down at the red notebook, took a deep breath, and—she talked. "I have to say this. My whole opinion changed. About boys. You really did the honor system great. And being quiet? Also great, everyone together. So . . . thanks."

And then the second hand pointed straight up,

and it was twelve fifteen, and the contest was over.

A yell went up that nearly peeled the tiles off the floor. Kids jumped out of their seats and ran and stood bouncing face-to-face with groups of friends, and everyone jabbered faster and louder than human beings ever should, laughing and nodding and telling everybody *everything* they were thinking and feeling.

And the louder it got, the louder everyone had to talk to be heard above the rising tumult, and the sound spiraled up toward that point where dogs run and stick their heads under a sofa.

And amid the burst of joy and noise and confusion, Lynsey shouted to Dave, "What's the official count?"

Dave nodded, cupped his hands around his mouth, and bellowed, "Forty-seven. Against the girls."

Lynsey looked at her notebook. She didn't try to talk—it was too loud for that. She turned the notebook around, and at the bottom of the page a number was circled. Seventy-four against the boys—a huge defeat.

Lynsey gave him an odd little smile, and Dave was ready for the teasing to begin. She shouted, "You didn't count?"

He was confused. "Count? Count what?"

Lynsey yelled as loud she could. "What I said, at the end."

Dave shook his head. "What?" The sound around them was deafening.

Lynsey flipped a page, and then turned the red notebook around so Dave could see it. And there was her whole little speech, written out word for word. The last word was "thanks," and above it she'd written a number: twenty-seven.

Dave nodded slowly as he stared at the speech and saw what Lynsey had done. He did the math in his head . . . *seven plus seven, and carry the one* . . . She had made the contest an exact tie—seventy-four points for each team.

And their private war? To see who got to label the other a loser?

Also a tie—her twenty-seven words matched the illegal ones he had yelled at Mrs. Hiatt.

Was it all too perfect? Of course it was. Had Lynsey messed with the score against the boys to make it add up that way? Without a doubt. Would there be a big investigation? Not likely.

Dave kept looking at the notebook. Lynsey's speech was filled with cross-outs and changes. She'd chosen those last words so carefully, making each one count.

He wanted to say, "I owe you, big-time."

He also wanted to say, "I guess I'm pretty much of an idiot, aren't I?"

And most of all, he wanted to say what she'd already said: "Thanks."

But Dave and Lynsey just sat there grinning at each other in the noisy cafeteria, and neither of them said a thing.

Not one word.